Soft & Rage

Myka Silber

Trash Panda Publications

Other Titles by Myka Silber

Individual Publications

Rider's Blood, Moonlit Black

The Pigment Thief

Anthologies

Unleash the Cosmos

(Nathaniel Luscombe & Jennie Sauer)

Unconventional Love

(Nathaniel Luscombe & Effie Joe Stock)

Sunshine, because it's written in a book it must be true: Hope may be the first step along the road to disappointment, but it's also the thing that makes life worth living.

Introduction

Most stories are about characters and events. The stories in the book are no exception. But they're also about places, regardless of their genre. The setting shapes them, lends them mood and atmosphere and substance to sink into.

Places and spaces are strange things. They are streams, flowing steadily — ever changing, but still the same stream. We experience places, we remember them, we dream of them. But when we return to them, they have completely changed — or perhaps it is we who have changed, rendering the place a stranger. Unrecognizable. Places can be characters unto themselves, building their own lives and stories. A dark house on a windswept hill under a full moon can be the boogeyman of childhood terrors, or a refuge far from the troubles of modern life. Or both. A place can be both home and prison, a place of peace and torment. A place where space and time are not quite what we expect them to be. A place that reflects character like a mirror. Whether magic, or merely a trick of time, some places become special.

This collection of tales crosses many genres, but is united by its emphasis on setting, and a taste for the magical and unusual. Historical fiction, fantasy, slipstream, and literary fiction all find their place here, with stories of grit and determination, longing, villainous intent, young romance, and descents into rage and despair. Pass through these written spaces, and take a moment to consider the places you travel in your life, and what stories they have to tell.

Sea Borne

It always started with the wind.

It would blow in from the sea and over the dark rocky headland, rattling loose shutters, making the trees sway like drunken dancers. The elderly would button up their coats and make for the indoors with a prayer to see the fishermen home safe. It was the kind of wind my Nan always said made the spirits restless.

When the wind comes to my door, it is a tamed beast, toying with the metal chimes outside the kitchen window. I know better than to be fooled. This beast is the herald of a gale — and so I do what all the women before me have done in this house: I light a white taper, place it on the window sill in the kitchen, then put on my galoshes and rain slicker.

My face ducked against the cold bite of the wind, I make sure the barn doors are secure, close the storm shutters over all the windows except for the one where the white taper burns. Satisfied, I sit down to wait under my porch awning. The frolicking wind always brings the sharp bite of brine, and the sweet promise of rain. I inhale deeply and remember.

When I was a little girl, my Nan would do exactly what I had just done. Then she'd scoop me up into her lap on the old rocking chair – the same one that had been on our porch since she'd been a little girl and the same one I sit in today. As we waited for the storm, she would take up my hair in her hands, her fingers deft from a lifetime of mending fishing nets, and she would plait it. Her soft voice would weave the tale of her brother as she wove a braid with her hands.

It was always the same story, the details exact, no matter how old she became. Her brother had been a fisherman, same as his da and his da before him, as far back as our family can remember. The way she would tell the tale, it would sound like our ancestors had sprung up from the earth itself right in this spot, and fished the sea ever since then. Our family has always survived on the sea, even when

10

others left and the trawlers took away livelihoods. A blessing and a curse, our uncanny ability to find fish where others found none. My Nan would say that the ocean was our blood, its salt in our bones. Our skin was the sand of the shore, our hair the dark kelp that pulled at unwary feet. The stormy sky brooded in our eyes.

The story was not about that though. It was about the last time her brother had gone out to sea. It had been late summer, and a freak storm had rolled in too quick. The boat had capsized, and despite his crewmates' best efforts, he'd been swept out into the deep. The survivors spoke of strange glimmers of light under the waves as my great uncle sank. Dark, lurking shapes. Just fish of course, but the story persisted even years later. He was claimed by the sea, a tithe of blood my family paid every few generations to the watery depths. The tale finished, my Nan would sink into her own memories while the storms howled. None of us would trouble her until the sun shone again.

Mainland ideas never quite took hold here. We laugh at the tourists who come here with cameras and legends in their heads hoping to see something other than rugged coastlines, dark copses of trees, and quaint whitewashed houses that have been here for longer than anyone cares to remember. In the deep of winter though, when the tourists are gone and the days are short, and darkness becomes our keeper — the locals flock together for safety in the warmth of the pub at the heart of town. Once they've been getting into their cups, they start to lean in, hunching their shoulders. They pitch their voices low and glance around like they're afraid of being overheard.

There's a hill with fingers of rock jutting up from the top that we don't climb after dark. There are faces in the trees that we nod to politely as we pass. We never look behind us when we walk along the shore in the twilight hours. We swap tales of times we'd been driving alone and felt like someone was next to us in the car — or when time itself had passed us by as a stranger.

All of us, whose ancestors might as well have sprung up fully formed from this wind-swept island, know that there are things out there that can neither be explained nor controlled by any amount of prayer. The land we walk on is old, far older than memory, and change comes slowly.

There are certain secrets that my family has never shared. Of course, it isn't actually possible to keep a secret on an island this small. The locals have whispered about us since time began, no doubt. They'll bid us good day, lend us a cup of sugar and do business with us; but they call us storm crows, spirit callers, and plenty more besides. My husband, a mainlander, laughed at the stories when he heard them. He told me that he'd always wanted to marry a witch.

A particularly large gust of wind pushes the hood of my rain slicker back, and I'm pulled from my reverie. Looking past the wooden fence that marks my land from the gravel road, I watch as the wall of rain approaches. It fills the potholes in the road within minutes, the puddles vibrating with every pounding drop of water that lands until they're overflowing, and the road becomes a river.

Finally, the rain rolls over my home, hammering the roof of the porch awning like a drum of war. The downpour veils my vision past the shelter of the porch. Now, it is time to prepare.

I push myself up, knees aching in the chill damp, and go back inside. My joints always ache with storms like these, and I can never seem to get warm until they pass. It's alright though, because I'm waiting for my husband to come home. Seeing him again makes up for anything else the storm may bring.

My galoshes go by the door, the rain slicker up on its hook. The cat curls around my legs with a questioning mew.

"I know, I've missed him too, Charity."

She sits down, looking up at the door expectantly. She's far older than a cat has any right to be. Her once brown fur is pale around her face, her hips don't work like they used to. My husband brought her home after one of his floatplane runs to the mainland. She'd stowed away somehow, and instead of taking her back to a mainland shelter, he insisted we keep her out of a sense of charity. So that's what he named her, and she slowly gained my grudging affection. It's been what — fifteen years now? She must be older than I am. She shifts her paws, kneading, anticipating the reunion.

I give her a quick pat and walk to the bedroom, the old floor planks creaking under me with each step. I shed my threadbare sweater, stained jeans, holey socks. I pull on the dress I reserve for reunions and funerals, a plain black garb that makes me feel twenty years younger. I roll stockings up my legs, taking care not to create runs in the delicate fabric. Then I go and wait by the taper in the window, watching the rain.

There's a triple rap on the door — my warning. My husband strides in immediately after, still in the warm wool coat he wears for late year flights. He stamps his feet on the front mat, a courtesy to my nagging about tracking dirt over my clean floors.

"It sure is comin' down out there," he says, rubbing his hands together.

"Welcome home," I say, approaching him to plant a kiss on his cold lips. I linger in the moment, remembering warm kisses of the past.

He smiles at me, and puts his hands on my bare shoulders. The cool touch raises goosebumps on my arms.

"You're all dressed up," he comments, but it's really a question. We always repeat this exchange.

"I've been waiting for you," I reply. "I missed you."

He laughs, and it fills the room. "I haven't been gone for that long, my dear."

I don't tell him that the last storm that brought him to my door was two months ago. I also don't tell him he hasn't been warm in years.

"I just missed you, that's all."

I gesture for him to come sit on the sofa with me. He hangs up his coat before sinking into his spot with a sigh. The sofa will smell like rotting kelp for days after this, but it's a small price to pay for a reunion. Charity hops onto his lap, purring, and nuzzles against him.

He tells me about his last flight. It's always the same story, the same sudden storm and the lightning strike that shorted his equipment. In his version, he always makes it safely to shore — a miracle. I don't tell him that his plane crashed into the sea, and his body was never recovered. He was supposed to be safe from the tithe my family pays — I thought I'd outsmarted it by marrying a mainlander who made his living in the air and not the sea.

I share the news of our grown daughter, run off to the mainland as far from briny waters as she can get — where she found a nice girl who doesn't believe in fairy tales and has no draw to the sea. Sometimes it's hard to remember what I have already told him. Sometimes I forget, and he looks puzzled when I repeat a story or neglect to tell him a key piece of information.

It always makes me wonder if in those moments he recognizes that something is wrong — if he starts feeling the tug of the deep before the storm has passed. The moment always passes though, and we laugh and joke just like old times. I don't tell him that I hope our beautiful girl will be free from her heritage. He'd just shake his head and tease me.

Sometimes he'll put on an old, scratchy cassette tape from our early days and we'll dance together. Even though he's cold to the touch, it's still nice to feel him there with me.

Up close, the watery smell of him wraps around me. If I close my eyes and lean my cheek onto his chest it feels like I've fallen asleep on a rock on the shore, and the breaths his body no longer needs are the murmured lapping of waves on a calm day.

Sometimes, there are rare storms that last days, where

we settle into a routine and it feels like nothing ever happened. My neighbours never stop by during these storms, and I've never spoken of these visits.

Today though, the pounding rain and roaring of the wind disperses too quickly. It barely feels like any time has passed. A child's tantrum, easily soothed.

My husband goes to the window where the lone candle still glows, restless. He licks his fingers and snuffs out the wick. A faint plume of smoke lingers where there had once been light.

"Storm's passed," he comments, running a hand through his dark hair.

"Yes," I say, my heart sinking. "It was a short one."

He turns to me, but he's no longer in the present. His gaze roams, looking for the sea.

"I think I'll take a walk," he says, "down by the shore."

"I'll come with you," I tell him, moving towards the door. "Let me put on my coat."

Somehow, his coat is already on. He waits for me, but his head is tilted to the side like a dog listening to a far-off call. When my boots and coat are on, he steps through the door, forgetting himself. I hurry to use the door to follow, as he's already striding down the walkway towards the road.

Outside, where the smell of the storm still lingers in the air, the call must be stronger to him. He doesn't seem to notice me anymore. His long steps make me rush to keep up. Despite my best efforts I trail behind him, forced to be an observer. As we draw closer and closer to the sea, he begins to lose his solidity. Once we're at the shore, he's no more than a faint shadow in the air, a half-forgotten memory of the man he once was.

There's no use in talking to him now. He won't acknowledge me – let alone know who I am.

I stay on the rocks as he steps into the surf. He wades through the shallows, the waves passing through his legs unhindered. I've watched this many times before, but I never feel prepared.

When he's up to his hips, the water rises around him. I've never really been able to describe the shape it forms. It's…. aware. But it doesn't really look like anything at all. Sometimes if I see it out of the corner of my eye it looks a little bit feminine, and jealousy twists my stomach. Then I blink, and it's just seawater swirled into a pillar. The pillar embraces my husband as he marches resolutely deeper, hiding him from my sight — seafoam and salt returning him home. I nod at the water, and it flickers faintly - sunlight under the waves. My Nan always taught me to respect the sea.

I stay until there's only the rolling surf, and a horizon as empty of my husband as is my life.

Transcendent

For moments of time beyond measure, you stare out the window, a wistful look softening your face. I always wonder what you think about in those moments where you are as unreachable to me as the moon, close but closed off in a cocoon of thought.

I asked you once and you looked me right in the eye and said you didn't think about anything at all — you communed with the world. I didn't know what to say. I'd never tried reaching out to the world with my self, attempting to connect with something larger than my own consciousness.

You asked me why I hadn't.

I told you I didn't believe in souls. Or God. Or any other overarching order to the universe.

You gave me a half-smile like you didn't believe me, and told me matter-of-factly that everyone has an essence, a spark carried within their flesh that is a small part of a greater living web. Your conviction made me wonder if I was missing out, but I couldn't bring myself to try.

I left you to your thoughts however — I did not want to intrude on those moments of pure serenity you achieved. In a way I envied you — your faith in a greater meaning to the whole. It might have been easier in some ways to live with that confidence.

Life went on. The stars continued traversing the night sky, fading into a pale dawn and a bright day, the earth turning around its axis as it hurtled at inconceivable speeds through nothingness, trapped in a loop by the physics of gravity around our burning star.

We were sitting in the car, the rain pounding on the roof and the slick black road as I drove down the highway, ten over the limit, heading north. Your hand reached out and slipped a CD into the player. After a moment of the windshield wipers faintly creaking across the glass and the pitter-patter of rain, the strains of violin filled the air, joined momentarily by violas and bass.

For a moment, I didn't breathe. The drumming on the roof joined with the stringed melody and synched with the swish of the wipers on glass. Time slowed to a trickle and the beads of water outside froze in place, and I felt as if I was adrift in a great sea of sound that swelled up and carried me away. I was still there, right there, but the entire universe opened up to me in one beautiful, perfect moment.

I breathed out softly and the frozen time shattered. My world reduced once more to the steering wheel, the road ahead of us. I glanced over to you and your eyes were closed, your hands held perfectly still in front of you, fingers posed as if holding something delicate. I understood you then, if only for the transcendent moment that slipped out of my grasp.

I looked back to the road and kept driving. Headlights blinded me like miniature suns before vanishing behind me, going the other direction. The wipers kept their steady rhythm, but the CD's melody never again quite matched up perfectly. I wondered if you had experienced that moment too, or if you had been caught in some other thread of the universe. We might have been caught together. Or perhaps we had both been alone.

Fast Car

It's fifteen minutes before noon, the end of my shift. Sarah is in the back putting her stuff in her locker, taking her time before she has to come out and tend the till. My 4am wakeup to get here has been weighing on me for a while now and time can't move fast enough.

It really is just like any other summer day, a relatively steady stream of travellers pausing to fill up their cars with gas, stretch their legs, use the facilities, maybe pick up a snack for the road. There are a lot of truckers too, hauling from one place to another.

I saw more of them when I worked the night shifts; the manager figured that since I was a guy, I could hold my own. I'm not sure who exactly he expected me to intimidate — I'm heavy, but it's not muscle. Anyways, that was before we hired Marlo, a burly man with enough tattoos to tell someone's life story. He wasn't from around here and brought a sense of worldliness with him. Sure, he'd never left the country, but he had thirty years under his very broad belt. He told me once that he'd lived by the ocean growing up, something I could barely dream of.

I'm barely paying attention, my mind on autopilot, just waiting for the last few minutes of my shift to end, when *he* walks in. I straighten unconsciously, tiredness just a lingering memory. He has a light tan, dusty brown hair, and he seems to have been formed out of the desert. With his hands shoved in his jean pockets, he looks around behind mirrored shades. I can't decide whether he should have eyes the colour of the sky, or of sage. Either would fit him perfectly as a creature of the earth, a traveller with no destination in mind.

He moves towards the drink cooler and I glance out at the gas pumps to see what he had come in. A dusty black Jeep is parked by a pump, its top down and a jumble of boxes in the back. I think I see a pan handle sticking out of one of them. He doesn't really seem to care about any of his stuff, the way the boxes are piled in haphazardly and held down with straps. I wonder if he even knows what he carries with him.

He strolls over to the counter casually with a bottle of coke in hand. With the sleeves of his shirt rolled up, I can see the delicate shape of the sinews in his arms and hands beneath his skin, and I have a sudden urge to trace them with my fingers, follow them up to their roots. He places the bottle on the counter and leans on his elbows lightly. I feel like he's scrutinizing me behind his sunglasses. I'm supposed to be the one who watches people — the passersby aren't supposed to notice me. Beneath his stoic gaze, I fumble through ringing up his coke. When I ask him if he needs gas, I have to restart twice before I can make the routine question come out right.

He smiles at me and pushes his shades up to nestle in his wind-tousled hair. Tilting his head to the side, he reads my name tag then straightens. "Samuel, is it?"

I nod mutely in response, caught in his eyes, which are neither blue nor green but a shade of both blended in with grey that reminded me of something I can't place.

"Pump #1, the jeep needs to be rung up."

I add it to the tally. "40.58."

I offer him the payment terminal, and he taps his credit card while somehow maintaining eye contact with me. It's unnerving, to say the least. He slips his credit card back into his wallet and flips the leather closed and pockets it. I hand him his copy of the receipt and his fingers brush mine as he takes it. The slight touch of heat is surprising. I hope he might come back another day.

I doubt it, but I'm drawn to him, in the way that I'm drawn to the road. He's somehow youth and freedom and life, all wrapped into one. The Stranger, the modern Zorro.

To my surprise, he extends his sinewy hand to me and says, "Sam, I'm pleased to meet you. My name is Riel." I meet his hand and shake it, my mouth dry. I have to clear my throat before I can force myself to reply. "It's nice to meet you too, uh, Riel."

I wonder if that's his full name or a nickname for something longer. It suits him though. I look down and realize I'm still holding his hand. Embarrassed, I pull away and look at his shoulder, unwilling to meet his eyes or see the smile I'm sure is playing on his lips. Covering, I clear my throat again and ask, "So, where you headed?"

"Oh, I don't know. Somewhere. I hear there are some great scenic walks in the area."

"There are?" I ask, puzzled. Ranch land and the orchards were inaccessible, and the monotony of sun scorched grass and small scrub is not what I consider scenic.

26

"You haven't been around much, have you?"

Damn him.

"Uh, well, one day maybe," I reply lamely, uncomfortable with my own shortcomings.

"Well Sam, this is a great opportunity for you to get out there. Want to come with me?" I glance up from his shoulder and catch a look of yearning before his smile returns. I almost feel like I imagined the previous expression.

"I dunno, I mean, I have to make sure my dad is okay, I really shouldn't…"

Riel leans forward and catches my hands in his, sending heat rolling up my arms. His eyes are magnetic as he murmurs, "Come with me Samuel. Your father is old enough to take care of himself."

I struggle to find the words to explain that I can't leave, that my dad is dependent on the bottle, that I need to take care of him. Instead, I find myself nodding, giving into the wingbeats of freedom hidden in his words. He lets go of my hands and steps back.

"Good. When do you finish?"

I check the clock. Where had my fifteen minutes gone?

How long had I been lost in thought, watching this man, this traveller, like an idiot? I glance to the back and sure enough, there's Sarah in her black polo and jeans, nametag carefully affixed to her chest, dark curls arranged around her shoulders.

"Now, I guess," I say, and I can see the curiosity in Sarah's face as she catches sight of us. I shiver slightly. *Us.*

I step out from behind the counter and head to the back.

Riel calls after me, "I'll wait outside," and I hear the jangle of the door bells as he returns to his jeep.

Sarah pauses me with her hand on my elbow and asks, "Who was that hot guy?"

"Riel," I reply and go to grab my stuff, shrugging off her hand.

"Ooh, looks like Sammy has a boyfriend!" she teases and giggles to herself. I'm glad she can't see me blush as I push open the door to the back room. In the relative solitude, I rake my fingers through my hair and wonder what the hell I'm doing.

I tell myself it would only be for a few hours at most, I deserve a little break, dad will be just fine and won't even notice my absence. There was always Mrs. Longston I could call to check on him for me, she didn't seem to mind. I like that she always smiles warmly whenever she sees me, even though I can never bring myself to call her Elise as she keeps requesting.

Folding my jacket over my arm, I take off my name tag and put it in my cubby. I take a deep breath and walk back out, waving to Sarah as I leave. She winks at me and makes a very suggestive hand gesture. I pretend I don't see it.

Walking out the glass door, my heart starts pounding when I see Riel look over and smile behind his sunglasses. Pretending that I'm calm and secure, I walk around the hood to the passenger side and climb in. I buckle my seatbelt and look at Riel.

"So where are we going?" Riel starts the engine, tosses his head with a light laugh before falling into a contemplative silence for a moment.

"Somewhere," he says finally, "anywhere."

I nod, as if I'm not in a car with a total stranger with no idea where I'm going. "Okay."

He pulls out of the gas station and onto the highway and I sink into the seat. I watch the dusty asphalt, grey with sunshine and cracked with age, flow by. The wind tugs at my hair and as we pick up speed the scrub brushes whip past us. I always liked watching the fences of the ranches, looking for the divides, searching for horses and cows and sometimes even llamas. It's been a long time since I've had the opportunity.

This stretch of highway is intimately familiar at first — I walk it twice a day along the gravel shoulder when I have a shift at the station. The nearest bus stop is 20 minutes away on a good day. Rain or shine.

As we speed along, my memory of the area becomes fuzzier, the landscape changing to one I don't know. The fences blur together and I find myself nodding my head, the sun a hot hand on my head, telling me everything is alright. The tiredness that had faded into the background rises back up and swallows me whole. I shrug my shoulders deeper into the seat and let my chin drop.

I wake up due to a warm hand on my shoulder. I jerk awake, completely disoriented and more than a little groggy. I look to Riel, who has opened the passenger door for me. Riel's got a camera slung across his chest. He smiles at me and hands me a bottle of water. "Here," he says, "you'll need this."

"Okay," I reply, wiping my face with my arm. "Where are we?"

"I found one of the walks I told you about. Shouldn't

take us long."

I hop out of the car and toss my jacket onto the vacant seat behind me. "I guess I'll be learning something new today then."

He laughs and claps me on the shoulder. "That's the spirit." I smile in return and follow Riel as he leads me away from the highway's gravel shoulder, along what seems to me like a goat path. Rocky and uneven, it leads around a small hill before starting up a gently inclined slope. Riel seems to slow his pace for me, letting me walk next to him rather than leading the way. We pause periodically while Riel whips out his camera and takes pictures of whatever catches his eye. I'm grateful for the breaks.

After half an hour, I'm sweating in my black polo. I stop and take a long drink of water before wiping the sweat off my forehead with the back of my arm. I can still hear the sounds of cars on the highway somewhere behind us, but it feels muted. I can hear insects buzzing, and the wind rustles the scrub all around us. Riel pauses and looks back at me, his hair gleaming gold with sweat and sun. "We're almost there, just a few more minutes."

I nod, too tired to answer, and take another drink of water. Tightening the lid, I take a step forward and unbalance on a loose rock. Riel throws out an arm and steadies me. "Careful," he says, and I'm embarrassed by my clumsiness.

He rakes his fingers through his mop of hair, slicking it back. With an encouraging smile, he says, "Let's go."

I sigh deeply and start again. What had started as a gentle tilt earlier has turned into a steep climb. The scrub brush offers no shelter from the heat as we walk, and I can feel the sweat rolling down between my shoulders, my jeans sticking against my legs. I feel out of shape and hideous while Riel seems to be in his element, a bronzed god of the land.

It's more than a few minutes before Riel stops. I glance over at him and find him watching me, his sunglasses pushed up into his hair. This time he doesn't smile when I meet his gaze, and instead gives me a look of yearning, the same I had caught earlier when he asked me to come with him. After a heartbeat, he looks forward and I follow his gaze. Instead of a dusty trail, there's blue sky. I realize that we're standing on level ground and I am deeply grateful.

"We're here," we both say.

I laugh, relieved, a little bit giddy from exhaustion. Turning, I can see the highway, all the rolling hills of ranch land interrupted by dark shimmering lakes, and neat rows of fruit orchards spreading outwards into a distant dark line of trees and mountains.

"It all looks so different from up here. It looks…. beautiful," I say, marvelling at the plays of colour on the land I had thought endlessly dusty and unbeautiful. Riel places his hand on my shoulder and looks out.

"Yes," he says. "I grew up on a ranch, and we had a big hill nearby. I'd climb it every chance I got, just to look out as far as I could. Makes you feel big, doesn't it?"

I nod. "Yeah, but small at the same time. Because you can't go everywhere, see everything, even if you want to."

Riel squeezes my shoulder in agreement and moves away. I turn in a small circle, taking in the rolling hills and the wide blue sky. Riel is unbuttoning his shirt, revealing smooth muscles under his golden skin that glisten with just the faintest sheen of sweat. I envy the confidence and strength he conveys, with the touch of grace that makes me want to watch him all day.

Putting his shirt and water bottle on the ground, he sits down and looks over at me expectantly. I walk over and sit down next to him, pretending that my heart isn't threatening to beat its way out of my chest.

"You'll cool off faster in the wind without your shirt," he says, "and it'll dry out too."

"Oh," I hesitate, "well…"

Riel brushes my arm with his hand. "Don't worry about it, you'll feel better without a shirt sticking to you."

"Okay." Averting my eyes, I pull my polo over my head and lay it out on the ground next to me, acutely conscious of how soft I am in comparison to this Greek god next to me.

I let myself lie back and tuck my hands under my head. I know dirt will be sticking to my back, but I can't bring myself to care. I hear movement and turn my head towards Riel. He's joined me in lying on the ground, his hands resting on his sculpted stomach. He's close enough to touch, and more than anything, I want to run my hands on his skin, feel the planes of muscle beneath. I let out a shaky sigh and look back up towards the sky.

The sky is hypnotizingly blue and the sun is a blanket of heat on my face. A gentle breeze plays over us and wicks the sweat off of my chest and arms. I take in a deep breath, smelling the dry grass and dirt. As I breathe out, my eyes flicker closed, and my mind follows the breeze away.

I relax until I might melt into the earth, a darker patch amongst the beige. I only slowly come back to myself when I pick up the sound of Riel breathing. Soft and barely audible, it reminds me that there's someone else with me.

When I open my eyes, I roll over onto my side, surprised to find that Riel is already in a mirrored position, his head propped up by his hand. His camera is in his other hand and I wonder if he had taken pictures while my eyes were closed. He smiles at me, warm and carefree, before asking, "How old are you, Samuel?"

"Eighteen."

"Shouldn't you still be in school?"

"I quit school when I was sixteen. Been working at the gas station ever since."

"Why?" He asks, before seeing how my face closes. "I'm sorry," he quickly adds, "I didn't mean to —"

" — no, it's okay. It doesn't matter. My mom left when I was thirteen, to find a better life. She was still young, you know, and beautiful. In her thirties, I guess. She still sends cards on my birthday, or calls, but she sounds happier wherever she is. Dad didn't take it well, got all moody and started drinking. At first it wasn't too bad, but then he lost his job 'cause he wasn't showing up to work and I had to do something cause our bills weren't getting paid so I… quit school. It's not like we could have afforded me to go to college or university anyways.

"Mrs. Longston, she was my history teacher, she didn't

give up on me though. She badgered me into keeping on part time, or doing distance learning. I finished high school, just on different terms than everyone else."

Riel's quiet for a long time. "I dropped out of university last year. I only made it through a year."

"Why?"

"I can't sit still that long. And being forced to read all these boring words from other people who've been dead forever. It's not me. I want to see things, you know? Experience life. I don't want to read about someone else doing things."

"I know what you mean. But for me? I'm trapped. Don't have anywhere to go."

"Have you ever seen the ocean?"

The change in topic startles me.

"No, today is probably the farthest I've ever been away from home."

"Would you like to?"

I laugh bitterly. "There's a long list of things I'd like to see, but I don't think I'm gonna be getting a chance to see them anytime soon."

"You could come with me. We could go west, to the coast. You could see it. The ocean, I mean." Riel sounds earnest, eager.

I sit up, looping my arms around my knees. "I can't. I have to take care of my father."

I can hear how bitter and resigned I sound.

Riel pushes himself up to sit cross-legged, facing me. "You don't owe that to him. He failed you the day you left school to take care of him. He's robbing you of your youth."

"He's my father. I can't just leave him."

"Yes, you can. You're eighteen. He is a grown man who needs to take responsibility for himself."

"What if something happens to him? I'd never forgive myself."

Riel shifts to kneel next to me, his knees touching my thighs. He reaches out his hands and turns my face towards him and I'm trapped.

I am aware of how close we are. How near his face is. My breath catches as I meet his eyes.

"You have done enough. Live."

Then he's leaning in and I'm leaning forward, and our lips touch and he tastes salty from sweat but I can't believe he'd want to kiss me and my jeans are suddenly far too tight. He pulls back after a moment, and I must look wide-eyed because he laughs. "Have you never been kissed before?"

"No, there's not, umm, people like me, here."

He strokes the sides of my face with his thumbs, before letting his hands drop to my shoulders. Impulsively, I raise my own hand to the back of his head and move in for another kiss, my fingers tangling in his sweaty hair. This time we don't speak, our mouths speaking without words, and Riel is pulling me in, our skin meeting and I think I might melt from how good it feels to have him holding me. Our sweat mingles together as does our breath and my hands are roaming across his skin, tracing the hard lines of his muscles in wonder.

Eventually, he pushes me down to the ground and his hands start to fumble with my belt. I freeze and my hands grab his. Riel separates his face from mine and he looks confused. "Do you not want to….?"

I feel a blush boom again. "It's just…. fast. You know?"

Riel relaxes with my words. "Oh, yeah, of course. Sorry."

He plants a gentle kiss on my lips and sits back. He rakes a hand through his hair and squints at the sun. "We should start heading back."

"Right, yeah." I get up and use my shirt to brush off my back. My lips feel swollen, but I don't mind. Riel pauses me right as I'm about to pull my polo over my head and snaps a photo. As I hold my shirt around my wrists, Riel shows me the photo he captured, and there's something about the light haloing me in the shot that makes me feel like maybe I'm not so ugly after all. It doesn't really feel like it looks like me, even though I know it is me. Just, some version of myself I've never met before.

When we're both in our shirts, we head back down and find his jeep right where we left it. We both hop in and Riel turns the keys in the ignition. We sit there for a moment, the engine idling, and Riel turns to me. "Please come with me. Please."

"This is crazy," I say, "we just met."

"Please."

I think of the photo and the way it looks like me but not me. A version of myself I'd rather be. I think of all the things I wish I could do, all the places I wish I could see. I think of the way Riel's lips tasted, the feel of him under my hands.

For a moment I consider my father, no doubt passed out on the sofa still. I then remember my mother's voice, the lightness in her tone over the phone with every call. I think I understand why she left, even why she left me. Other people hold us back, weigh us down. I glance at Riel. But maybe they can also set us free.

"Okay. But we need to stop by my place so I can pack a bag."

Riel smiles and it lights up his whole face. "Whatever you want, Samuel."

and the stars were in her hair

I fell in love with her the day she shone as brightly as a star.

It was one of those university Halloween costume parties where all the girls try to wear as little as possible. I was a pirate, a quickly cobbled together costume with an ill-fitting wig and hat, and the vest and faux boots were comically falling apart. My cleavage is safely tucked in, my legs covered. I wasn't expecting her to show up, she'd said she'd have to think about it.

I leaned against a wall and sipped my rum and coke and pretended that I was having a good time, and ate far too much of the brightly-wrapped candy in the bowls placed around the room.

It was hot, it was crowded, and everyone was far more drunk than me. Being the sober one at these kinds of things just makes it seem ridiculous, and people watching becomes a depressing exercise in realizing how fake some of them are.

It was close to midnight when she swept in. Her dress was palest blue, with a net of pearls and sparkling clear gems overtop. Her dark hair was caught up in a delicate crown of silver stars, and her bare neck was regal. The crowds parted for her, for she glowed in this room, demanding space without speaking a word.

I drifted towards her, tugged into the gravity of her orbit. My pulse raced, my hands were sweaty.

"I thought you weren't coming," I said.

"I wanted to make sure my costume was finished," she said, and her smile lit my insides as brightly as a sun.

"It's incredible. You're incredible." I may have sounded fervent. A disciple meeting their deity.

She laughed and shook her head, touching my shoulder with her warm hand. "You're drunk."

Perhaps I was more drunk than I realized. Or maybe

I was just intoxicated by her presence. But I knelt down in front of her, taking her hand in mine. I kissed her knuckles, my lips pressing against her smooth skin. I looked up at her, and there was a strange look on her face. With her halo of stars, she was otherworldly to me.

"My lady of stars, dreamlike wonder, most beautiful of all, may I ask for one wish?"

A faint smile tugged at the corners of her lips. "What do you wish for, scourge of the seven seas?"

My heart fluttered. "A kiss of your starlight."

She blushed and it was the prettiest thing I'd ever seen. "Yes."

I rose to my feet, cupped her face in my hands, and stepped in close. Our lips met and my eyes closed as her hands settled onto the curves of my hips. For a moment in that stale room, I was transported into another world.

Werifesteria

This far out of town, the air tasted like smoke from the farmers burning their leftover straw from the harvest.

Deacon closed the door of his vintage Mercedes and inhaled deeply, his lungs filling with the sharp autumn air. This was his favourite season, always had been. Everything just seemed more possible in the many shadows of the shortening days.

A faint smile tugged at the corners of his mouth as he slung his camera bag across his chest. He'd parked his Mercedes by the side of the road, just short of an old-school wooden bridge crossing a small river, halfway between nowhere and the middle of nowhere. Right where he wanted to be.

He picked up his rifle from where he'd rested it, locked the car and pocketed his keys. As he surveyed the quiet road, it occurred to Deacon that by all rights he shouldn't be standing there under the shade of the oak, maple, pine, and birch. He should, instead, be living up the image of himself he cultivated, of the Ivy League prep-school boy whose unshakeable confidence in his trust fund made him cool without trying too hard. Everything from his hair to his clothes to his shoes and his car screamed it.

He paused, lingering in the sunlight of the road, thinking of the classes he was missing. He shrugged it off — it wasn't anything a smile and a casual mention of his father's name couldn't fix. It had gotten him out of trouble many times before. The best part was no one would ever bother to check in with his father, and his father was happy to ignore Deacon so long as he passed his college classes.

With long, easy strides he left the road and went in amongst the trees. Here, the sunlight was muted, a fiery canopy of leaves sheltering the forest floor. Every step he took was marked with the crunch and crackle of brittle leaves. He was hunting, it was true, but his quarry would not be scared off by the noise.

If anything, he hoped the noise would attract it.

If not, he had patience. His hunt had not started today, or even this week when he had read a news story in some disreputable rag of a magazine of strange sightings in these very woods. Instead, it had started twelve years ago on the night his mother had reportedly vanished. Deacon knew better, however. There was no coming back from where his mother had gone.

His father had been away on business, as he often was. His mother and him had stayed up past his bedtime, watching scary movies that would fuel his dreams for weeks, because he'd asked and she'd had a good day and was feeling indulgent.

It was towards midnight when they'd heard banging outside the house. Deacon's mother had frowned, told him to stay put, and went to look out the French doors that led from the kitchen to the sprawling rear of the family estate. His mother had opened the door and stepped outside, looking towards where the trash bins were stored.

What had followed next had been the source of speculation for months. According to the police report, his mother had been kidnapped after a struggle, the blood stains and gouges in the grass explained as his mother's attempts to get free. What the newspapers said was that the wife of a wealthy investment banker was missing after a bloody struggle, publishing leaked images of the shredded lawn behind yellow police tape.

The newspapers spoke of the eight-year-old son who had been the only eye witness, and some more intrepid reporters had tried to interview him at school or accost him on the streets until his father had threatened to file complaints. Then they backed off.

After the novelty of the event wore off and no sign of his mother had been found and no ransom note was received, it had moved from the front pages to the back pages, and then finally to the gossip rags that insisted JonBenet Ramsey was alive or that her killer had finally been arrested.

Deacon had desperately wanted to tell them what he had seen. The police hadn't believed him; his father hadn't believed him. They chalked it up to trauma, a coping mechanism. Believing that a wolf that walked like a man had grabbed his mother and dragged her away under the light of the full moon was too far-fetched for any of the officers who had responded to his 9-1-1 call. Or for his grieving father who could barely look at his son.

The memory, however, was imprinted in his mind. He had watched every agonizing second of the brief fight, where his mother had done her best to fight the monster that had dared encroach on their backyard. He'd listened to the snarls, the screams, and the final silence. Only then had he been able to move from his frozen post of observation, to run to the phone and call for help.

His father had cancelled the rest of his business trip and flown home and waited for a ransom request or a report that his wife's body had been found. The waiting consumed him, leaving no time for a young son who spoke of monsters and myths.

Neither news nor ransom came. Deacon kept trying to convince his father of the truth, of the terrible truth that they were not alone in the world, but failed again and again. He knew that the only thing they would ever find of his mother would be bones scored with deep grooves made by hungry teeth.

When his father lost hope and would no longer tolerate any mention of his wife, Deacon was sent to boarding school. He was required to see the school counsellor once a week until finally he stopped trying to convince everyone else of the truth he knew. He came to the realization that his word was not good enough, that he would need proof. So, he silently promised himself that he would be the one to show the world how fragile their reality was, how there was so much more out there.

It would be his secret, until he was ready. Deacon

learned to pretend and did what his father wanted. He got good grades. He played sports. He got into Dartmouth College. Perhaps not in the subject his father wanted, but he was there as a cultural anthropology major. It allowed him to use his personal research into cryptids and the supernatural to fuel his papers.

Of course, he never claimed that he believed in them; instead, he used his interviews and evidence to analyze the psyche of the American people, how the stories of the unknown were used by locals to keep norms, to explain the unexplainable, to grapple with humanity's limited understanding of the universe, to hope for something beyond tangible reality.

Despite three years of searching, he had yet to find concrete proof, something that was so clear and so unarguable that he would be able to prove the existence of the supernatural once and for all. Today, however, was as good a day as any to find proof. Today, his quarry was the Appalachian Black Panther.

His camera was for capturing evidence, his rifle a dose of reality that he was hunting a predator.

As he walked, he had to admit that perhaps the counselling had done him some good. He should have been sweating, anxious about coming face to face with something that could tear into him much like the beast that had killed his mother. And yet no flicker of memory surfaced as he walked in the dappled sunlight. It was like that night had been another person's life, or something he'd seen on TV. No nightmare reared its head.

It was just him, the crunch of leaves under his feet, the bunch and stretch of his leg muscles, the weight of the rifle in his hands held at the ready.

He walked until the sun had peaked in the sky before pausing to take stock of his surroundings. He was now in the thick of the trees and the smell of smoke had been replaced with the living smell of a forest. He inhaled deeply, closing his eyes and tilting his face up to the sunlight that filtered through the leaves. Warmth bathed his face and he found himself smiling. Blinking his eyes open, he rolled his shoulders out and turned in a slow circle.

He listened intently, hearing nothing but the fluttering of leaves and the creaks and groans of trees breathing. No hint of a rumbling purr or leaves cracking under heavy paws. With a sigh, he pulled his phone out of his pocket and checked the time. The white letters blinked at him, letting him know it was time to turn around. As much as he wanted to spot the mythical black panther, Deacon wasn't willing to do it in the dark where every step could lead to tragedy.

He swiped the screen on and opened up the GPS-enabled map. After a moment, his phone picked up signal and a blue dot blinked into existence. He turned until he was facing the road he had left and then pocketed his phone. Hands once again weighed down by his rifle, he trudged back towards the road, his stomach grumbling at him that it had not eaten since a hurried bagel and coffee that morning.

The path back felt longer, or maybe it was just that disappointment made him slow his steps in the hope that if he took long enough the Appalachian panther would appear. He started focusing on the leaves at his feet, kicking them into small bursts of colour in the air before they settled back down. The repetitive motion lulled him into a trance and he lost his earlier sharp focus. It wasn't until a flash of black zipped across the edge of his vision that his head snapped up and he froze, his heart pounding and his mouth dry.

He raised his rifle to his shoulder in a practiced motion, his eyes scanning for the animal that had startled him. Finally, his eyes picked out a squirrel half-way up a tree, sizing him up with one eye while it shook its tail in agitation. It was perfectly caught in the crosshairs of his scope and he could bring it down with barely a thought.

Instead, he breathed out slowly, lowering his hands and slinging his rifle over his shoulder. Trying to be as quiet as possible, Deacon took out his camera and popped the lens cap off before raising it to his eye with slow, steady motions. The squirrel darted onto a branch and he followed it through the viewfinder. When it had settled again, chewing on something it held in its front paws, he focused the lens and snapped a picture.

Even if he hadn't found his proof, he'd still leave with another shot for his budding photography portfolio. Laughing at himself, he stowed the camera back in its bag, raised his middle fingers in salute to the squirrel, and kept walking back to his car with a spring in his step.

As he unlocked his car he took one last look at the woods, noticing the way the cold sun lit everything up as gold. One day, he told himself, he would find his proof. And then everyone would believe him about what had really happened to his mother.

No Pocket Can Hold Forever

I've lost my way. I can feel it. The way the air itself feels wrong, changed. The sharpness of the sky. The slight skew of colours that tells me I am not home.

This is an in-between place. Somewhere between hello and goodbye, good night and good morning. A pocket of time held still. It's not a bad place, really. Anything you can imagine can happen here. But it's not real. Or at least not real in the meaningful sense. Nothing actually changes here — no actions are permanent.

It's a safe place to rest, for a while. It can become dangerous though. If you linger here too long it can lull you into complacency. You'll live, but won't truly be alive. Some people need that though. The peace of it, I mean. Some hurts are too much to bear, some cuts too deep. If what you need is forgetting, then the pockets are a place of healing.

Those people don't often leave the pockets though. They get trapped by their own need to escape the pain. They can't learn to live with it, to move past it. I leave them be. Their pockets felt intimate, personal, when I've stepped into them by accident. I always get out as quick as I can. I don't like getting blasted with someone else's emotions.

This pocket isn't that though. It's empty aside from me. I'm trying to find a way to close it — its edges are bleeding into concrete time and it is starting to cause distortions. Pockets do that sometimes. Appear rogue in the middle of busy intersections or in a classroom or an office tower. It ends up becoming a major inconvenience and necessitates a rescue operation to get people out of the pocket.

Obviously, scientists have found a way to create small, stable pockets that you can pay to rent or own. It's quite the premium price to pay for the privilege though. There are also rogue operators who go about with stolen tech to open pockets for all sorts of reasons. Those are the worst. They always feel a little bit oily when I enter them, more wrong than usual.

Anyways. I got sent to take care of this pocket. It

had appeared in a courtroom during a murder trial, which obviously could not be tolerated. The initial emergency rescue of the terrified jurors had already happened, so I got sent in to clean up the mess.

It's not a bad gig, closing pockets. I get to work solo — my word is what goes. My boss knows better than to tell me what to do — he just tells me where and how bad. It can be a little inconvenient though. I never know when John's going to call. Always have to be available. Hard to take a vacation, you know?

Some people assume just anyone can be a Closer. To a certain extent, that's true. The tech we use isn't that hard to learn, a week of training and just about anyone can use it. But there's a difference between knowing how to use the tech, and knowing where and when to apply it.

You can't just step into a pocket and turn the tech on and expect it to work. You need an affinity for the pockets. You gotta be sensitive. At least, that's what Magda said when she tested me as I sat in the hospital outside Jenna's room. She was a bit more into the woo-woo stuff than I was ever comfortable with, but she was also right about this. You have to be able to feel the pocket, find its resonance point, not let it suck you in. It'll show you whatever you want to see, and that's the danger of being a Closer. The bigger the pocket, the harder it is to resist.

This one is a doozy. I'm not sure how long I've been inside it, or even where the edges are anymore. I'm well and truly lost.

There's some sort of scientific explanation as to how pockets appear to people. That it's not the pocket adapting to the person, it's the person's own neurons trying to process the anomaly of the pocket. Typically, this will present as the most comforting memories the person has. Then again, there's the sick fucks who use pockets to live out their twisted power fantasies of murder or worse. That's a controversy I don't care to comment on. It might be harmless, but maybe people shouldn't indulge their darkest urges to hurt others. Won't have me on the record saying that, though.

Nope. Layla Stephens, Closer: No comment. Makes my life easier.

In any case, whether it was the pocket or my neurons, I'd already walked through happy childhood memories, the one Christmas as an adult where no one had argued and we'd all gotten drunk and sung carols well into the night, my first date with Jenna in the sunlit café where I would later propose to her. That one hurt. I wanted to linger there, drink in her smile and her magnificent laugh. Her loss is still an ache. Thirty-two is too young to be a widow. Jenna was the best thing that ever happened to me and it is entirely unfair that cancer took her away from me.

I knew better than to linger in that café though. No matter how much I wish otherwise, that place with the rich smell of coffee brewing and the thick velour armchairs was just a memory and I needed to keep going.

The café fades into a new place. Somewhere unfamiliar. The walls are a cheery yellow, there's a big window with gauzy white curtains, a rocking chair and a dresser and a crib. Jenna stands by the window cradling a baby in her arms. I freeze. She turns to me and smiles, her cheeks dimpling. "Hey babe, how was work?"

"It was good," I say automatically.

Jenna approaches and she smells faintly of milk and sweat and I could cry. I kiss her cheek and she hands me the tiny bundle that is the child we never had. "Peter's been a bit fussy today."

I bounce him gently, gazing into his small face, his mouth a round 'o' in sleep. "He looks just like you," I comment.

Jenna laughs, putting a hand to the remnants of her baby bump. "I did spend nine months growing him, I'd sure hope I'd get some credit."

I bite my lip to keep from sobbing. Delicately, I hand

the baby back to my dead wife. "I'm sorry, I have to go."

She frowns, puzzled. "You just came home. Can't you stay?"

I shake my head mutely. There are no words.

I bolt. The world around me is indistinct for a moment, a haze of colours like an oil slick on water. When I stop, lungs heaving, I'm in a sunlit meadow, bees lazily droning as they land on the profusion of colourful wildflowers.

I let out a scream, tilting my head back and clenching my hands into fists. When there is no more air left to push past my lips, I collapse to my knees and let out the tears.

Pockets always show me memories. I was used to that. I wasn't expecting it to show me a future that could have been. A future I'd been robbed of.

I stayed in that meadow until the tears were through, the sun a benediction of warmth on my head.

I feel hollow afterwards, empty of all feelings save a determination to finish this job and get the hell out. My legs are a bit shaky and I have to dry my cheeks on my sleeves, but I stand up and start walking. The meadow, surprisingly, stays with me. There are mountains on the horizon so I head towards them, no better direction to follow.

After a while, it becomes apparent that my instinct was right. I start finding chairs, sheets of paper, pens, a purse, a shoe — all are incongruous in their surroundings.

Finally, I reach it — the heart of this pocket. The colours are all too bright and tend to shift if you're not looking directly at them.

I slide my backpack off and assemble the stand and the box. I fiddle with the antennas, checking their tuning. When they're configured correctly, I flip the series of switches that activates the Pocket Harmonics Destabilizer. Or PHD as we normally call it.

I feel when it starts to work. All my hairs rise on end as the vibrations fill the air. The pocket squirms for a moment and I tilt an antenna just-so to compensate. There. Perfect harmonic resonance.

The pocket fractals into a kaleidoscope of colours as it collapses. I've always found the death of a pocket beautiful. It contracts until I'm standing in an empty courtroom in disarray.

Quietly, efficiently, I pack up the PHD and shoulder my backpack. I pause for a moment in the empty room, remembering Jenna's smile as she held our son. Gone, again.

Sergeant Daniels pokes his head through the door,

interrupting my reverie. "All clear?"

"Yup, it's safe now."

He visibly relaxes and steps into the room. "Took you longer than normal."

"Mmm," I comment back. I don't know him like that.

He looks like he wants to ask me something else, but can't make up his mind. Finally, he settles on, "Where are you off to now?"

"I need a drink," I comment and walk past him. "Call me if another pocket shows up."

"Right. Thanks Layla."

"Anytime, Sgt. Daniels," I say and wave as an afterthought.

"You can call me James," he calls to my back.

"Maybe one day," I say back, and then there's a door firmly separating us.

I get waved through the police lines easily. The officers all know me in this city. I've closed enough pockets for them at this point. I always answer the call, no matter when or where. The city's most dedicated Closer.

It's a relief when I'm outside in the rain. Something I

know my mind did not create. Something real. I let it soak through the shoulders of my sweater, drip down my face. Reminding me that I made my way out. That my grief hasn't taken me yet.

Fish in the Trees,
Wolves in the Sea

She drifts into wakefulness. The dawn is pale, soft —
dreamlike, a pastel kiss of colour. Weak sunlight touches her
eyelids and she surfaces, eyes opening.

The water is chilly this time of year, but it braces her
and rocks her tenderly. Her lips taste of salt, and as she
looks around, the ocean is silver-grey, calm.

A hunger tugs at her. No, not hunger. Aching emptiness
— longing. Something missing.

She lets the waves push her to shore, all pebbles and
rocks. They shift and clack under her feet as she straightens,

examines this sheltered cove. Yes, very familiar. She's come here many times before.

There were smiles and laughter in golden honey sunshine, tears in the rain, kisses under the endless starry sky and the pale smudge of the milky way. Memory is gentle, ease.

This cove is not where she is meant to be, however. She climbs the beach to the thick trees.

Here, the space feels enclosed. Thick tall trunks surround her, moss hanging from branches in strands, sprays of green needles shutting out the sky. Even the sound of waves upon the rocky shore is dampened here. It's quiet. A different kind of cathedral, just as sacred.

She steps on the bed of fallen pine and fir needles, the softer browned shoots of cedars. Ferns and boulders hem her in, keeping her to the narrow trail she has walked many times before. Small streams of water cut her path on occasion and pine cones litter the ground, but she steps over them without thought.

Her feet are bare, so she weaves a path to avoid the sharp rocks and scratching bark of fallen branches.

Eventually, the trail comes out to a road. She hesitates here, looking both ways down the single lane strip of dark grey. Something surfaces in her mind, screams and violence. She shakes her head, letting the memory go. There is something else today.

After a moment, she decides. A tug of memory calls to her. She turns to the left and walks down the side of the road, the shoulder of packed dirt.

The occasional car whizzes past her, their passage whipping her hair into her face. She continues on, resolute. She ignores the cars as much as they ignore her.

A faint memory surfaces, a conviction that the people here used to slow down for her when she hitchhiked on this road — offered a lift into town. It's a small place, after all. There are no strangers here.

She keeps on.

The dawn is well past, the sky clearing to a brilliant blue, when houses start appearing along the side of the road. She names the inhabitants by force of habit.

Mrs. Smith, the grade school teacher whose daughter Jenny had gone to law school and never came back. Mr. and Mrs. Chen who owned the only Chinese restaurant in town. Mr. Rivers, whose garden hadn't been looked after since his wife died of cancer. And more. Not so many as there used to be.

Children grew up and moved to better jobs in the city. The old died. The lumber camp workers never stayed long. Sometimes the forest cut them down as they cut the ancient trees. Blood for sap — a trade.

Not everyone could leave, however. Some were called to this place of transformation, a birthplace cradled by cedars and ocean brine, where wolves could take to the sea and salmon landed in tree branches. The wild coast.

She had been called. She still felt it — the drumbeat pulse of it. No matter how far she went, she would always return to this place. Her home.

It takes some time, but she arrives at the timber house, its roof overgrown with moss. She walks up the gravel drive, the front door swinging open easily at her touch.

She drifts from room to room, but no one is home. Not yet. There is a glass of milk left out, and she thinks it had been very kind of her sister to remember. She drinks it, the hollow ache in her chest disappearing. Humming happily, she repays the favour, running through the daily chores: vacuum, dust, dishes, wash the kitchen and bathroom, tidy the toys from her niece and nephew.

Content, she takes up a perch on the kitchen counter, kicking her legs freely. A warm glow lives at her core, and it is almost time.

Her sister comes back first and stares at the surprisingly clean home. Dear Tammy, with her beautiful black hair shining in a cascade all the way down her back.

Tammy sees the empty glass of milk on the counter, turns to look around. She calls out hesitantly, "Sis?"

Yes, sister. She drifts to the heart of her heart, presses her lips against Tammy's cheek and wraps arms around her. "I will always take care of you."

Tammy shivers, withdraws, folds her arms across her chest, eyes wide. "We miss you Sam. I love you."

Sam. That is her name. She'd forgotten. "I love you too, Tammy."

Tammy walks away, deaf to her words, and Sam resumes her perch on the kitchen counter.

Her niece and nephew spill in later, dropped off by the school bus, tussling each other about who got to pick the movie that night. Sam smiles. They were getting bigger with every breath.

Joe and Mary pause when they pass Sam's spot on the counter.

Mary, younger by two years, smiles and waves at Sam. "Hi Auntie!"

Joe frowns and smacks Mary's arm. "Who you talking to weirdo? Auntie Sam went missing years ago."

Missing? No. The ocean and forest had embraced her.

There was a flash of memory, of screaming and pain and a knife. Sam pushes that away. That's not important.

Mary points at her aunt, and insists, "She's right there!"

Joe shakes his head and snorts. "You're seeing things."

He looks troubled however, like the corner of his eye is catching sight of things that he believes shouldn't be there.

Sam hops off the counter and kisses the tops of their heads. Little Mary kisses Sam's cheek, and excitedly runs off to tell Tammy that Auntie Sam visited.

The hollow in her chest is full and she no longer aches. Sam drifts out of the house, retracing her previous path down the road, a soft glow of warmth lighting her. Something feels unfinished, however. Something she still needs to do.

Part way back to her cove there is a young woman standing by the side of the road with a large bag. Clearly waiting. Memory tugs at Sam and she slows.

The young woman's face is vaguely familiar, but no name comes to mind. Sam stops and takes up position next to the stranger. Sam will wait too. Sam remembers waiting just like this.

It isn't long before a pickup pulls up and the young stranger hops in. Sam climbs up too, settling between the stranger and the driver. John, one of her high school classmates. He's losing his hair, she notices.

He's smiling, but memory of his features contorted in anger crosses her mind. Something is off.

John begins driving, asking the young woman questions. Her name is Sarah, she's going to see her boyfriend one town up. Her parents don't approve because she's eighteen and he's thirty-three. John fills in details of his own life. He's divorced, his ex has full custody of the kids, claims he hit her when he drank. A lie, of course, according to him.

Sarah shifts uncomfortably in her seat, her eyes flickering from side to side. Her fingers are pale where they clutch her bag.

They get to the pull-off for Sam's cove trail and John slows down. He asks Sarah if she has ever gone down the trail and she says she hasn't.

John says they should go, it'll only take a few minutes. The light is fading fast. Sarah says her boyfriend will be upset if she's late, her voice shaking.

Sam puts a comforting hand on Sarah's shoulder. The young woman isn't alone.

John parks, shuts the engines off, pulls the keys out. Sarah's fingers scramble for the door handle and she spills out onto the side of the road, bag in hand, nearly falling but catching herself at the last moment. Sam follows, memories intersecting with reality. She's been here before. Anger sparks.

Sarah is running, but she's too slow with her bag and it's getting tangled in her legs. John tackles her to the ground. Sam advances on their wrestling figures, watching Sarah scream and flail at John to let her go. He's calling her a bitch and a whore, and telling her to hold still like a good girl.

Sam freezes, remembering John's face blocking the sky as he tears at her jeans, telling her she's a stupid bitch who had put out for every other man in their town, so why not him?

Sam's hands clench into fists as John fumbles with his belt buckle. Anger is heat, sparks flying. She flies at him straight as an arrow.

Her rage pours forth from her in a primal roar, for herself, for Sarah, for every other missing or abused sister.

She slams into John, her hands sinking into his chest,

grasping his heart. He freezes, gasping at the sudden icicle shoved into his chest. With a scream, Sam rips out his heart, holding aloft the bloody offering that pulses in her fingers.

John collapses onto Sarah, who shoves him off of herself and scrambles backwards, staring open-mouthed at Sam. Sarah can see her, can see the heart ripped clean from a chest.

"Who, who are you?" the young woman asks, trembling.

Sam considers the question for a moment, letting her arms fall to her sides, her hands painted red. "This is my road. I eat the hearts of bad men. You're safe now."

Sarah nods, her cheeks still wet with tears. She grabs her bag and starts backing away. Her voice shakes as she says, "Thank you."

Sam turns, no longer interested. The sense of something unfinished has left her. She takes a bite of the heart she has claimed, the tough muscle still hot. Chewing, she passes the parked truck, its driver door open, and drifts down the forest trail.

By the time she has reached her cove, she has finished the heart. A sense of peace washes over her. The sun is setting and she pauses for a while to watch the sky and sea be painted in vibrant golds and reds and violets.

As twilight takes the sky, Sam wades into the waves. With the last light of the day fading beyond the horizon, she lies down in the cool embrace of the water, letting it rock her.

Somewhere below her, a jumble of bones picked clean by fish rests in the murk. Sam closes her eyes and sinks down into sleep until the next time she is needed.

A Place to Rest

Her hands were filthy, dirt making the white crescents of her fingernails black, mud splattered on her skin up to her elbows before blending in with the black rolled-up sleeves of her shirt.

Focused, nearly frenzied, she continued digging with her hands, widening a hole in the soggy earth below her. If all had gone well, she should have had the help of two other sets of hands, and shovels. Instead, she could hear the ripples and snaps of mage-blasts and the less unsettling sounds of metal and wood clashing.

She paused, panting, sitting back on her haunches. The rain pelted her face and lightning flashed across the sky.

Some distance away, someone screamed.

It had taken her months of research, a few bloody interrogation sessions with key persons and a midnight heist of a map to figure out the location of this unmarked grave. The information had better be correct — it had taken her months of work to get here and she didn't want it to be for nothing. She had planned this night in great detail and she wouldn't have an opportunity like this again for a long time.

Rolling out her shoulders, she ignored the fight nearby and continued moving the black earth until her fingernails scraped against wood. She widened the hole, splinters of wood shoving themselves under her nails. Wincing, she kept at it.

When the hole was wide enough, she stood from her crouch, muscles screaming in protest. She kicked the wood with the heel of her boot as hard as she could. It needed a second blow, but splintered in. She hoped she'd calculated right as she threw herself back down to the ground and blindly reached into the hole she'd created.

Her hands, slick as they were, slid over a jumble of smooth, angular rods that she knew were bones. Her mother, she knew, would forgive her trespass. She thrust her arm in further, lying flat in the mud, her fingers skittering now over cold silk. Finally, they settled on something cold, hard, and smooth.

With a small cry of victory, she wrapped her fingers around it and pulled her arm back. Getting to her feet, she looked at the green-black gem on a gold chain she held in her hand, the pendant that was her birthright.

With the pendant clutched tightly in her hand she ran towards the on-going fight. Her two helpers this night, Didier and Romain, were swinging their shovels at a mage guard who was doing his best to fend off the two would-be grave diggers with snaps of palest blue power from his hands. With a sigh, she drew on her own reserve of power and flung it at the three of them at once. There was a bright flare of violet from her fingers towards the guard and her helpers who hadn't noticed her arrival.

Then, as one, their necks snapped at unnatural angles and they slumped to the ground.

Her breath curled in front of her face, the only sound now the pouring rain on the bare branches of the trees in this small wood a short drive from the nearest outskirt of Paris. This inconspicuous place where the French kings buried the dead they did not want found.

She turned her attention to the gem and breathed a flicker of her power into it. It flared a vivid green, twisting her own power into something new, but familiar to her as her own breath. She watched in triumph as the spirits of the three newly dead men rose from their bodies, pale and translucent. They stepped out of their corpses and bowed to her, awaiting her command. King Louis XX would regret having executed her parents and forcing her into hiding shortly after the turn of the new millennium.

She was Amarante Guilleroi, the last true psychomancer, and she would make Paris tremble with her spirit army. It was, after all, built on bones.

There was one last task for her here, however. Amarante stalked back to the hole she had dug in the earth and the gem in her hand flickered once more with power. A fourth spirit rose up from under the earth, dressed in a beautiful silk gown, hair perfectly coifed, jewels sparkling like frost crystals against her dark hair.

Amarante bowed to this spirit and fed more power into the gem, giving this spirit the ability to speak. Her eyes still lowered, she said, "Maman."

Ma fille, what are you doing? The spirit asked and Amarante raised her eyes.

"I am avenging you and papa, for what the king did to you."

Her mother had the audacity to look disappointed. After

everything Amarante had suffered, had done to get to this moment, anger flared in her chest. "The King cannot be allowed to live."

You do not understand the power you hold; it will consume you entirely. Forget your vengeance, go live somewhere where you can be at peace, her mother urged.

"There will be no peace for me until the King is dead," Amarante snapped and held forth the gem. "Goodbye maman."

The gem dimmed for a moment and the spirit sank back down into the earth. Her mother held out a ghostly arm towards her for a fleeting moment, a look of anguish crossing her face.

Amarante gritted her teeth and swiped her muddy sleeves across her face, brushing away angry tears. Of course her mother was not proud of her. She had never appreciated her too-clever daughter. Amarante would show her. She would show all of them how much they had underestimated her.

She pulled the pendant chain over her head, letting the gem settle under her soaked shirt. Its greenish glow was muted, and Amarante held a hand over it for a moment, feeling the new weight of it. Finally hers — this power that had been owed to her since her birth.

She set off towards the road, just a short walk away. The three spirits she had raised followed her obediently, faithful companions in death. It seemed stupid to her that the royal family had chosen for centuries to bury their hidden dead here, leaving only a meager handful of mage guards to watch over them. Amarante stepped over the first mage guard who had died that night, ignoring his glassy-eyed stare. Pathetic.

When she reached the road and her parked motorcycle, Didier's car right behind it, she paused and considered. The unwanted dead, were they? Well, she had a use for them. Amarante turned and pulled the gem from under her shirt and held it in her hand. Exhaling, she funnelled her power into it. She wasn't sure exactly how many dead were buried here, but she wasn't about to leave potential minions here.

The dead mage guards rose first, most freshly dead. Other spirits followed more slowly. Except her mother. Amarante couldn't bear to see that face in judgement.

An ache formed behind her eyes as hundreds of spirits rose from their unmarked graves, in clothes that ranged from modern to ancient garbs she couldn't place in time. Silent, they stood facing her, their eyes upon her. Amarante smiled — her army was forming.

Turning her back to them, she let the pendant drop

under her shirt once more and kicked her leg over her motorcycle, settling onto the damp leather seat. She fed it a small spool of her own magic, not the gem's, and the engine roared to life.

She kicked it into gear and guided it forward. She glanced over her shoulder, and her spirit army moved along with her. Perfect.

She accelerated rapidly, eyes squinting against the rain that pelted her face and head. She could hear the wind rushing past her ears, whipping her long dark curls back. The drive back to Paris was easy, quick, weaving between cars as her spirits floated along behind her. The bike's engine was a comforting purr, and she and the machine moved as one along the roads.

She made her way to the 14^{e} arrondissement, to the Place d'Enfer. A fitting name, Amarante thought, as she pulled to a stop and rested her foot on the curb, the bike's engine idling. Her spirits circled around her, and she could hear pedestrians screaming and running away. Good. They should be afraid.

Amarante pulled out the gem and held it tightly in her hand. She closed her eyes and poured as much of her power as she dared into the gem, the gem flaring vividly even against her shut eyelids. She directed the gem's powers down, under the cobblestone streets, into the hidden tunnels that had become a tourist attraction.

The ache behind her eyes deepened into a throbbing pulse in her skull and an echoing ache began in her chest, but she ignored it, pouring magic into the catacombs where six million dead had been moved. Fools. They had gathered together everything she needed for her army.

When she opened her eyes again, squinting against the pouring rain, all she could see was spirits rising up from the ground, waiting for her command. Her grin was feral as she kicked her bike back into gear. One last stop and vengeance would be hers.

She drove north, her army a wave of spectral forms streaking after her, crossing the Seine to the 9$^\text{e}$ arrondissement. She skidded to a halt outside the Palais Garnier, the golden statues on its roof gleaming in the artificial light. The Opéra. Where the King and the entirety of his court would be, along with the glitterati of Europe, for the premiere of a new ballet. Her face twisted into a sneer at the thought. This would be their last night of enjoyment.

She cut her motorcycle's engine, kicking out the stand and sliding off smoothly. She looked around her, and she could no longer see the ground in the plaza it was so filled with spirits. Amarante threw back her head and laughed. How the King would cower before her now.

Mage guards were descending the stairs, crying out in alarm, but she barely paid them any mind. She pulled out the gem and ordered her spirits forward. Completely silent, they moved as a single-minded unit, crashing onto the mage guards like storm waves. The screams of the guards were cut short as the spirits sucked all the life from their bodies.

Amarante strode forward, ignoring the twitching bodies of the guards as their spirits silently rose up and joined rank with the specters who had killed them. The gem still clutched firmly in her hand, she ignored the throbbing pain in her skull and her chest and climbed the stairs to the Palais. Throwing open the doors, she sent her army flowing through, killing everyone in their path, regardless of who they were. If they were here, they were just as guilty of her parent's murder as the King.

Her army flowed through the halls, cutting short screams of terror as they descended upon their victims, the dead rising to join their ranks. She came to the auditorium at last and flung open the rear doors. The ballet was still on-going and the lights were down. Her spirits glowed ghostly green in the dark, as they flowed down over the seats and floated upwards to the balconies.

The symphony of screams was a delight to her ears as the audience were set upon by the spirits. Some tried to run, but her army was too many and her will was too strong. It was a feast of terror for several minutes and Amarante stood there gloating as the rich and famous joined ranks with her army.

The King, however, she left for last. The spirits surrounded him, holding him in place, as around him one by one screams were cut short by death.

As the audience joined her army, Amarante felt her limbs become heavy, leaden. Exhaustion washed over her as more and more spirits fell under the gem's control and she needed to pour more of her own magic into the pendant to keep them chained to her will. Gritting her teeth, she climbed up the stairs to the royal balcony. Her vengeance was almost complete, she could hold on until then. Her heartbeat felt erratic, and every breath brought stabbing pain as she laboured up to end the King.

After what felt like long hours but in reality was mere minutes, she stepped into his balcony. He cowered against the railing and she could smell he'd pissed himself. Good.

"Who are you?" He stammered. "What do you want?"

"Do you not recognize me, majesté?" she sneered.

He shook his head, trying to make himself small. Despite his fine clothes, Amarante was unimpressed by what she saw. He had worn glamours when he appeared on the news, that she knew. But to see him here, stripped of everything, she scorned his weak chin, the blonde curls that were thinning, the watery pale eyes. He was pathetic, pitiful, and yet he had killed her parents who had been strong and proud. She sat down heavily in his seat in the balcony, her limbs too tired to hold her up any longer.

"I've waited a long time for this day, you know," she said conversationally. "You executed my parents. I vowed I would get my vengeance on you and it took me years to get here. But finally, finally, I have you where I want you. My name is Amarante Guilleroi, and I sentence you to death."

His eyes widened with recognition at her name and a thrill of pleasure ran through her leaden body. Good. He would know who had done this to him and why. She sent a last drip of power into the gem and the spirits fell upon him, ripping at him, snarling at him, as he screamed in terror and flailed at them. Satisfaction flared in her chest as finally her revenge was complete.

His spirit rose, gazing at her mournfully. She could barely keep her eyes open and her hold on the gem was difficult to maintain. She slumped down in the seat and tried to release the spirits, but the gem had become molded with her hand and it was glowing too brightly. It had latched on to her power and it was feeding on her, draining her magic from her veins.

She struggled weakly to get the gem away from her, desperate for this not to be the end, but in doing so she let her will wander and the spirits were no longer chained to her. Amarante looked up wide-eyed as the army she had created, that she had dreamed of for so many years, turned on her and descended upon her like ravens on a fresh kill.

As they tore at her, she roared, defiant to the end, the last true psychomancer.

The Firebird and The General

She trailed embers like dust, bright flickers in the dusk from the ghostly flames that made the train of her black dress. She walked serenely through a pocket of silence — the soldiers hushed one another and drew back in fear as she passed by.

Battle, death, blood — these they knew. But this creature was magic, and old magic at that. They covered their eyes and prayed her gaze would not fall upon them.

The ground was churned to mud between the tents and cookfires, but she glided along as if it were some grand marble hall. The muck did not sully her dress or cling to her soft slippers, as if it too was afraid to draw her eye.

She stopped at the largest tent of this army encampment and the two guards posted at the entrance dropped to their knees and bowed their heads to her. *Ensure we are not disturbed*, she said, her voice high and musical. The guards bowed lower, acknowledging her words but not daring to speak.

She brushed the tent flaps out of her way and stepped into the warmth of this tent. Her hands began to weave invisible strings as if playing a children's game before she sent her palms wide. The tent walls, previously white, now glittered red and gold and deep purple, a magic net woven into the fabric.

A red-haired man who had been absorbed in maps and missives looked up at the sudden movement. His eyes widened and his face went pale. He stepped away from the desk and bowed deeply at the waist but said nothing.

General Vorace, she said, *the Wolf King has sent me to congratulate you on your recent victory.*

Vorace straightened but did not look up from the carpeted ground. *His majesty is most kind. My victories are in his name.*

She drifted closer, circling the tall, broad-shouldered man. *Do you know who I am?*

He stiffened. *The Firebird.*

Yes, she said thoughtfully. *One of the king's magic birds, with my sisters the Stormhawk and the Iceswan. Glittering ornaments of his court.*

She paused directly in front of the general and tilted his chin up with a delicate finger so that he would meet her gaze. His eyes were grey and he had a full beard, as red as the hair on his head. His nose was broad and crooked from a break that had not healed properly.

He met her liquid dark eyes steadily but she could nearly hear his pulse fluttering in his throat. *There are other, cruder, names they call us.*

The King's Whores, the general said, but his cheeks coloured red with heat.

She let his chin go and the corners of her dark red lips curved into a smile that died before reaching her eyes. *Yes, that one.*

She swirled her dress and glided over the carpeted floor of the tent, surveying the plain furniture, the evidence of dedication to work, the iron braziers lit with dancing flames. The Firebird contemplated the tent in silence for a long moment before turning back to the general. *The Wolf King wishes to reward your loyalty with a night in my company. I have put a silence barrier up. No one will hear.*

The general's eyes widened and his hand rose to comb fingers through his beard. *I.....His majesty is too kind. I am not worthy.*

The Firebird paused and tilted her head, her flames brightening. *Do you not desire me?*

How can a mortal man desire a dream? Such things are beyond us.

She smiled cruelly. *Do you refuse the King's gift?*

He hesitated. *I could never refuse his majesty.*

She drifted closer and placed both hands on the sides of his face. His eyes flickered between hers but he made no move to draw back. The Firebird leaned in, her red lips parting, and she kissed him slowly. His eyes closed but his hands stayed at his side.

She pulled back, voice smoky. *What do you want of me?*

The general shook his head minutely, his jaw still trapped in her hands. *I could not ask anything of you. I would sooner ask a star or the moon. What is it that you wish to do? If his majesty wishes you to be here in my company, how might I serve you, my lady?*

She recoiled, releasing his face. Her flames flared up,

then quieted to near invisibility. *I have not been asked what I wish in many, many years. I wish…*

The Firebird began to pace the tent. The general sat back down at his table, watching her. After a few moments she slowed, then glided to the general's table and took the chair opposite him. *Do you have a chess board?*

He looked surprised but nodded.

I would like to play chess with you, the Firebird said, her expression soft.

The general exhaled softly and rose to his feet to retrieve the game from a plain wooden trunk. *I do not play frequently.*

No? she questioned. *I would have thought with a mind for battlefield strategies such as yours, you would greatly enjoy chess board stratagems.*

The general paused with the game box in his hand, looking down at the simple object thoughtfully. *Chess is the strategies of court intrigue, uncaring for the pawns. I deal in calculations of lives lost, lives taken. A great general preserves his soldiers.* He looked up and blinked, remembering his company. He bowed to the Firebird. *Forgive me, I mean no offense.*

She laughed then, the tinkling call of birdsong. She

gestured a delicate hand. *Come, sit. Let us play, speak freely. It is refreshing to hear honesty, general.*

A look of relief flickered over his features before they settled back to neutral. He sat back down, placing the game board between them and setting up the carved wooden pieces. *As you wish.*

She hid a smile behind long fingers, watching the care with which the general placed the carved wooden pieces. They were simple, pale maple and dark walnut, the marks of the tools that made them evident. They would not have looked out of place in a simple farmer's cottage. The Firebird picked up a knight, rolling the piece in her fingers. *Who made this?*

The general did not look up. *My father.*

The late Lord Jobin Vorace made these? I did not know he was a wood carver. The general's hand froze, hovering over the board with a pawn in hand. *No. He was not.*

Ah, yes, the bastard son was raised by peasants before Lady Vorace died in childbirth with yet another girl. Then the son was sought out and brought to his father, so the father might have an heir.

The general carefully placed the pawn down but he was frowning. *Lord Vorace was no father to me. My father was a wood carver, my mother a maid. I was fourteen when the Lord came for me and claimed me as his property.*

The Firebird raised an eyebrow. *Are you not grateful to have been raised from nothing to a lord, and the opportunity to become one of the most decorated generals in our nation's history?*

The general raised his eyes, anger colouring his expression. *I did not ask to be ripped from my home, and a family who loved me, to spend years mocked for my poor manners and backwards ways. My name will always be Thulin Carver to me. The victories I have earned I earned for love of the people of this nation, not for glory or power or the might of the King. I will protect our people.* He snapped his mouth shut and stared at the Firebird, his hands trembling.

She simply nodded. *Do not fret, I am the King's pet, but I only share the information I care to. What you say here is safe with me. I understand what it is to feel used.*

The general released a shaky breath and finished setting up the board. *Black or White?*

White.

He nodded and spun the board so the pale wood faced the Firebird. They set up their opening moves in silence, their actions deliberate and considered. After a few moments as the game began in earnest, the general asked, *How is it you came to serve the throne?*

The Firebird smiled sardonically. *That is a long story.*

We have time, the general said. *We have all night.*

The Firebird shrugged, a surprisingly human gesture from her. *Then let me tell you the tale of a young foolish girl. There was a young maid long ago, who lived on a small farm and tended the chickens and sheep, whose head was full of stories of wonder and adventure. She wished more than anything for magic, to have power to leave her poor existence. But what could she do in her small village? There was a woman who mixed herbs to heal ailments, but it was small magics, and the girl wanted more than such paltry tricks.*

She wanted silks and jewels and grand halls of marble, she wanted to be a princess, and she dreamed of it whenever she could. The day came where a young man from the village asked for her hand in marriage, and she thought she could never imagine herself wedding him, or anyone else from the village, for to marry was to be trapped. So she packed a small bundle and set off deep into the woods where it was said a witch lived, a legendary creature of old, who could grant any wish, for a price.

The young maid found an old hut, abandoned with time, filled with crystals and herbs and bones. She was hungry and cold for winter approached, so she made herself a home in the woods. She read the books, and learned some small magics, but it was not enough. Then came a day where men came with spears and fire, having heard of a witch in the woods returned, and they did terrible things to the young maid, leaving her to die next to the smoldering remains of her hut.

She vowed that day she would become so powerful that no one could ever hurt her again. She lived, and she searched for all of the knowledge of magic she could. Years passed and she came one day to caves as old as the world, filled with water that had been the seed of creation. The guardian of the caves warned her that there was a price to the power she sought, and the greater the power the greater the price.

Heedless, the woman drank from the water and her very veins hummed with power. For a glorious moment, she was free, a creature of flame and feather, terrible and beautiful to behold. But the guardian spoke true — the price was steep. The woman was no more, her name ripped from her, and given to the throne of our nation, so that the Firebird might serve lesser beings. The Firebird was bound, body and soul, in service of the line of kings and queens, and so she lived for long decades, a golden jewel in the crown of the monarch, unageing in her pretty cage.

Her voice faded away and the only sounds in the tent were the crackling of the fires in the braziers and the gentle clink of the wooden pieces as the two players continued their game. After a moment, the general asked, *Is there a way to break free?*

The Firebird hesitated. *Perhaps. There are three seals in the royal treasury that hold the true names of my sisters and I. If the seals should be broken, and the names released to us, we would be free.*

The general folded his hands on the table in front of him and frowned at the board, seeing that the Firebird had cornered his king and he would lose. *What would you do if you were free?*

The Firebird's dark eyes glinted and her expression became feral. *I would burn the Wolf King in his palace with all his jewels and lords, and rain fire upon the heads of the lords and ladies who plunder the land and take from the people.*

And then?

I do not know. It has been so long that I have lived in a gilded cage that I can only dream to burn it down.

The general tipped over his king, surrendering. *I hope one day you will find the freedom you desire.*

The Firebird inclined her head and began resetting the board. *And you? What will you do when your fighting days are over?*

The general shrugged. *I do not know. The Wolf King commands, and I obey. That is all. I dream, sometimes, of a quiet life in a cottage in the woods, where I am merely a man who crafts wood into items, but that is a dream that cannot be.*

The Firebird hummed softly in response. *Again?*

The general nodded. They played quietly into the night, the Firebird's flames dormant, the general no longer thinking of the battles to come.

The Wolf King's Hall was darkly glorious — no human hand had wrought the dark twisting pillars, the impossible angles, the fanciful glass walls that told of his glory. Sound distorted, sometimes carrying to the far end of the room, sometimes becoming whisper quiet. It was said, sometimes, that the King knew where all these distortions were and would manipulate the courtiers to place them at best advantage to himself, depending on how much trust he placed in them. He did seem to have an uncanny ability to ferret out plots against him — only fools would believe themselves safe to speak treason in the King's Hall.

The general walked down the center of the grand hall, ignoring the soft chatter of the courtiers clustered in knots to see the returning hero. His beard and hair were freshly trimmed and oiled to a soft sheen, his clothes of fine cut and cloth. A cape with the king's emblem embroidered in gold thread sat on his shoulders, waving gently with every step. His boots clicked on the polished marble floor as he walked but he held his head up, his gaze fixed solidly on the far end.

There stood the Tangled Throne — a mass of iron strands woven into a seemingly delicate seat, the back of the seat imitating the roots of a great tree, cushioned in blue velvet. At its feet was a series of steps with cushions in a riot of colour and on them perched the King's magic birds in various poses of repose. On the left, the Firebird, flames of her dress dancing, studying the courtiers with a bored expression. On the right, the Stormhawk, her pale dress as sheer as mist, lightning arcing across the fabric in bursts, her eyes fixed intently on the approaching general. The most beautiful of the three, the Iceswan, sat straight-backed, her dress the palest blue, frost gracing her hair and skin in fractals, her gaze fixed at something only she could see over the heads of those gathered in the Hall.

The general stopped at the bottom of the stairs, and knelt down on one knee before bowing his head in reverence. He stayed there, motionless, waiting for the cue to rise, not even daring to breathe. Heavy footsteps came down the steps and the general closed his eyes for a moment, before a heavy hand rested on his head in brief benediction. *Rise, General Vorace.*

The general rose to his feet slowly, coming eye to eye with the Wolf King. He was a mortal man, it was true, but one would be forgiven in sensing deeper powers in him. His face was handsome, with chiseled jaw and high cheekbones and eyelashes that would be the envy of any blushing maid. A thick beard and dark curls graced his head and he was taller than most, with broad shoulders and a trim build. His clothes were the richest black, embroidered with gold thread. His eyes, however, his eyes were what caught others — they were yellow, predatory, calculating. The Wolf King watched his general now with those eyes, not missing any details.

Your Majesty, the general said simply.

The Wolf King smiled, but there was no warmth in it and it did not reach his eyes. *A most triumphant return. I congratulate you on your victory.*

The general bowed his head in thanks. *The victory is not mine, but yours.*

The Wolf King barked a laugh, revealing sharp canines. The general said nothing, keeping his face impassive.

Tell me general, how may the King reward your loyalty?

You are most generous, your Majesty. I can think of no reward I could ask for.

The Wolf King circled the general, hands folded behind his back. *No lands, no gold, no wife, no lover? Is there no gift you desire?*

The general for a moment met the gaze of the Firebird. A fleeting flash of concern passed over her features before she returned to studying the courtiers.

My duty is enough for me, said the general.

Does your duty warm your bed at night, General Vorace? the Wolf King asked, quiet titters of laughter answering from the courtiers.

The general flushed but kept his gaze steadily on the throne. *My duty takes me away from my bed for long times. A cot is my most constant companion.*

The Wolf King paused his circling and stood facing his general. He appeared lightly puzzled, his head tilting to the side as if there was a mystery he intended to solve. The general met his yellow gaze steadily, hands steady at his sides.

A feast then, the Wolf King declared, turning in a circle to smile at his courtiers. *A feast to celebrate our Kingdom's victory, and to toast our most humble general.*

There were a few cheers from the crowd and the Hall filled with clapping. The general inclined his head as the Wolf King slapped him companionably on the shoulder. Ice settled along the general's spine, but it was not from the magical bird who sat watching him with white-frosted eyes.

The general heard a quiet knock on his door and he paused in adjusting his doublet. *Come in.*

Soft-slippered footsteps followed the arc of the door and the general turned from the silver mirror to look at who was disturbing his dressing for the feast in his honour.

When he caught sight of the pale blue dress, he bowed immediately.

General. My sister sends a message. Choose a prize, or choose death. Every man must have a price.

The general looked up but she had vanished, only a trace of glittering frost remaining on the wooden floor where she had stood, which quickly melted. He ran a hand through his hair, letting the words sink in. He turned back to the mirror, doing up the last of the buttons of his doublet before cinching on a belt. No one could bear arms in front of the king, so the belt sat lightly. He walked through his chamber in the palace, one he rarely spent time in, his eyes skimming over the heavy furniture and décor he had not chosen. His eyes rested finally on the plainly carved chess set on a side table and he smiled faintly to himself.

Later, he drank steadily, forcing himself to smile and laugh with the courtiers who surrounded him, asking him for tales of battles and how their sons might learn under his tutorship. He did not speak of the blood and the mud, the slog, the screams of the battlefield and the medical tent, the scent of burning flesh, the waiting for doom and the release of action. He instead spoke of the bravery of his soldiers, which of his officers had showed exemplary leadership, the follies of his opponents.

They fawned on him, mothers urging their eligible daughters to cozy up with him and hang onto his every word, but the general was not interested in their perfumed hair and glittering jewels. He played his part, but he felt the eyes of the Wolf King on him, measuring him, weighing him. The night stretched out, harps and tambourines and fiddles playing dance tunes, the courtiers whirling riots of colours in the Wolf King's Hall. The general smiled at every request to dance, claiming to have two left feet. He was left to watch the festivities, nursing a strong ale. The Wolf King swirled amongst his courtiers, tall and elegant, sometimes dancing with one of the ladies, sometimes taking one of his glittering birds to the floor, a pocket of room opening up around them.

It must have been well into the night hours when the Wolf King sat down next to the general and poured himself a cup of ale from a jug. He took a long drink, and leaned back with a sigh of satisfaction. *So, my most loyal general, are you certain there is no boon you would ask of me?*

The general inclined his head, the room spinning

slightly, his body suffused with warmth. *The war has ended. The managing of a lord's estate has little appeal to me. Perhaps, you would do me the honour of being in your personal guard?*

The Wolf King's pointed canines flashed as he said, *A most interesting request.* The King ran a heavy hand through his beard silently. *No,* he finally said. *I have no guards; I need no guards. Perhaps, however, you could watch over something much more precious to me. My birds — you could ensure their safety.*

The general blinked, then nodded. *As you wish.*

Mistake me not, General Vorace, they will tell me of your doings and you will tell me of theirs. You may regret not retreating to your lands to caretake them.

The Wolf King took a long drink of ale, patted the arm of his chair affectionately, then rose to rejoin the revelry. The general no longer felt warm, but chilled to his very core.

Days blended into months and years. The King's birds stayed unageing. The general's hair became streaked with silver, fine lines appearing around his eyes, the corners of his mouth. He was no longer a general but in name. He stood guard outside the King's birds' rooms, accompanying them when they left the palace grounds, their silent shadow. He dared not speak to them, nor meet their gaze for any length of time. Sometimes the Firebird would place a burning hand upon his arm and he would remember a night in a tent playing chess and he would smile quietly as she passed him by.

The sisters, as the general thought of them, spent much of the time in their wing of the palace, reclined on cushions and chattering about the various members of the court, the latest fashions, artists and bards they thought might be worth sponsoring. They never spoke of the Wolf King, nor of the young women they had been before being trapped into his service. He learned that the Firebird enjoyed chocolates, the Iceswan loved to dance, and the Stormhawk could paint beautiful scenes. The general began to know their footsteps by heart, their particular unearthly scents of woodsmoke, the first frost of the winter, and the smell of the air after a lightning strike. Which of their laughs were genuine, which were false.

Sometimes they would be summoned to the Wolf King's chambers and whichever bird was chosen would be silent and withdrawn for days after, her sisters huddling around her for pitiful comfort. Worse, in the general's mind, was when a bird was sent to a courtier's chambers or estate, a token of favour sent to please. The general ground his teeth but stayed silent as he travelled with the chosen plaything. He began to leave small carvings for them where they could find them on these occasions, small wooden animals or hair combs or boxes for their jewels and powders and perfumes. They said nothing, but sometimes he would catch the sisters holding his crafts, soft looks on their faces. They began to invite him to sit with them instead of standing by the doors and to walk in their inner garden sanctum with them.

The general learned how they took their tea, their preferred foods, and began to direct the servants on what they should bring the King's birds and when. The Wolf King laughed at this, calling the general the caretaker of his birds, no longer a warrior. The general bowed his head, letting the laughter buffet him, keeping his peace as the King lost interest in the general who was content to fade into obscurity.

The courtiers mocked him in the halls, forgetting that he had once been hailed as a hero. The general simply smiled at them and brushed them aside. What they did not know was that in the chill of the first touch of dawn he practiced his sword drills, the blade an extension of his will, keeping his skills quietly. What they did not know was that he learned the palace like the back of his hand, the servants' halls and the grand rooms until he could pass as a ghost from wing to wing.

◆ ◆ ◆

The general stood in the royal treasury room with a dark hood pulled up to cover his face. Blood was on the hem of the long cloak and splattered on his boots, but he did not notice. He did not have much time, but it would have to be enough.

He searched through the rows of gold and gilt and glittering gems; fluted crystals and priceless tapestries and ancient artifacts. When despair began to settle on his chest, he came upon what he searched for — a plain black wooden box that smelled of magic. A scent that had become as familiar to him as his own name. When he flung upon the lid, nestled in the green velvet lining were three ivory seals — one engraved with a bird of flame, one engraved with a bird clutching lightning in its talons, the last with a bird of winter frost. His hands trembling, he picked up each seal. One by one, he snapped them in his strong hands. Inside each was written a name on a piece of parchment.

Hoarsely, he said, *I name you all three: Vanya Riven, Beala Tritan, Shayle Ban, and return your names to you.*

The parchments crumbled to ash in his hands and he stepped back. For a moment, there was only silence. He let out a long breath, his empty hands falling to his sides as the fullness of his actions hung over him. Briefly, he wondered if he had perhaps misunderstood what would happen - then he heard screams in the far distance.

His legs long, he ran from the room, his cloak flapping behind him like a banner, his sword sheath slapping his leg as he ran. No one took notice of him, chaos reigning in the palace, as three unearthly birds swooped and shrieked, tearing the palace and its inhabitants apart.

He reached the stables where a plain brown horse was already saddled and waiting for him. He swung up onto the gelding's back and spurred the horse away, away, to the edge of the palace grounds and then through the city, letting the horse find its gallop stride.

Finally, when he was outside the city gates, he turned for a moment and glanced back over his shoulder. His hood down, his hair had grown long and wavy, the red streaked heavily with grey. He saw a trail of fire in the sky, diving down once more, smoke rising from golden wings. He placed his hand over his heart and said, *I wish you peace.*

A wood carver sat on a log outside his cottage, an axe leaned up against the doorframe next to him. Humming, a pipe clenched in his teeth, he whittled away at a piece of wood, drawing forth an image only he could see in the grains of the wood.

He looked up at the sounds of leaves crunching underfoot and was surprised to see a woman, her dress a dark grey, her cloak a rich red. Her hair was black and fell in waves around her shoulder, her eyes were liquid black, her lips a dark red. His joints creaked in protest, but he lowered himself to one knee and bowed his head, setting aside his carving and tools. *My lady.*

She laughed and it was the sound of the first birdsong of spring. *Rise, Thulin Carver. You need not bow to me.*

Painfully, he lifted himself back up onto his seat and brushed long silver hair from his face. *I did not think I would see you again. You are just as beautiful as when I first laid eyes upon you. Freedom agrees with you.*

She approached and laid a gentle hand on his shoulder. Her lips moved in silence and Thulin straightened with wide eyes. He stretched out a leg experimentally and looked up at her face in wonder. *Thank you.*

The woman crouched down and placed her hands on his knees that no longer ached, smiling warmly into his age-lined face. *You returned my name to me. I am Vanya once more. It is I who must thank you, for the gift of freedom you granted my sisters and I.*

I'm sorry it took me so long, he said, resting gnarled hands over top of her delicate knuckles. *I am happy to see you again.*

I hoped I might stay awhile to visit an old friend. Perhaps play a game of chess or two, she said, rotating her wrists so that she could grasp his hands in her. Her skin radiated warmth, a banked fire burning under her smooth skin.

Thulin smiled. *I would be honoured to host an old friend. Please, come in, I can put on a kettle of tea.*

He rose on newly young legs and held out his elbow. Vanya wrapped her arm in his, and let him lead her into his cottage. Open stairs led up to a loft and the main floor was a kitchen with table, and armchairs by the hearth. Shelves of books lined one wall and thick woven rugs were scattered across the wooden planks of the floor. Everything was plain but well made and Vanya smiled at the memory of a previous meeting place that had been similarly furnished. She sat at the table, watching as Thulin hung a kettle over the fire and produced mugs for tea.

He hummed as he worked, placing tea before the both of them and producing a familiar chess board.

Have you learned to play any better since last we played? Vanya asked teasingly.

I told you once before that I am no good at chess and the years have not improved my game, I'm afraid.

You seem content, she commented, looking around at the cozy home. *Have you found the peace you were looking for?*

He nodded, opening up the game board and setting out the pieces. *This is what I dreamed for myself. Have you found a new dream for yourself?*

Not yet, Vanya said. *My sisters and I are now the caretakers of the people and we cannot leave such responsibilities. But I had a small dream, of visiting a friend and forgetting my cares for a while.*

Sometimes small dreams are the best, Thulin commented. *What colour?*

White.

As you wish, he said, turning the board so that she could start.

Vanya smiled. What she did not say was that many, many years ago the guardian in the ancient caves had told the Firebird that the seals that held the names of her and her sisters could only be broken by one who loved them but did not desire to control them. She did not say that she remembered a general who had shown her kindness and who had loved his people and his land. She asked instead about his life as a woodcarver, the village where he lived, his life.

They played for long hours and he cooked them dinner, and when the light of the fire grew dim, he insisted she sleep in his bed while he curled up in blankets by the hearth.

The next morning, when he awoke, he found that Vanya had left in the night. On the pillow where she had slept lay a wooden carving of a bird of flame, rising from its perch in flight, so delicately carved it looked like it might flap its feathered wings, that its flames danced in the breeze.

Thulin smiled as he picked up the small statue and tucked it into the pocket of his vest, so that it might be close to his heart as he went about his day.

No Glory in Remembrance

The hill wasn't anything special. Just a hill, really. But when I crested the peak, there was a pile of boulders that eons ago had been set at the top and formed a very convenient sitting spot. Years and years of fires had darkened one side of the boulders, evidence of this being a favorite place.

I perched on top of the boulders and remembered why Tilley had loved this place so much. The view was glorious — the forest valley and then the sharp peaks of the snow-covered mountains, rising high above our heads like ancient gods. It had gotten difficult for her to come here the past few years. Her joints had ached and old wounds had pulled in a way they hadn't when she was younger.

We had sat here many times, long days turning into long nights, discussing everything there was to discuss and then more. I had watched her, year after year, show signs of age. The grey hairs, the wrinkles, the eventual retirement from a life of adventuring. Her swords hung up over her mantle as a reminder. She still could draw her bow though, all the way to the end. She was proud of that.

There had been a sudden slowing down, so strange to see when I had known her to be vibrant and full of life, but I knew my human friend had reached the end of her candle. It didn't seem like enough time. It never seemed like enough time. Sixty years had passed for her, and yet I looked the exact same as the day I met her. Elven blood was no gift at times like these.

She had made me promise that when she died, I would collect her ashes and bring her here, so that she could enjoy this view forever. Who was I to refuse such a request?

I had stood by the funeral pyre, silent, as the human villagers spoke of the strange woman who would disappear for months or years and come back with stories of far-off places and battles and dragons and treasure troves of gold. Of the elder who dispensed wisdom to any who would ask. They honoured her. I could not speak — she had been beautiful in battle, an excellent companion on long hard roads, but that is not what I remembered. I did not mourn the myth — I mourned the reality. Her laugh. Her wit. The way she would inhale the steam from a fresh mug of tea before drinking it.

There's no glory in these things. But they were precious treasures to me.

Slowly, I opened up my pack and pulled out the urn that contained all that was left of Tilley. When the wind picked up, I carefully opened the container and tipped out the ashes in a thin stream, letting the wind scatter her across the hill.

When the ashes were dispersed, I held the urn to my chest for a moment and whispered, "Goodbye, old friend."

Root-Found

The asters were humming quietly and the anemones were bobbing their heads in the breeze, petals happily reaching for the midsummer sun. Cilia was sweating under her broad straw hat, but it was a good sort of sweat, the sweat of labour done with gladness. Her garden was in bloom and it mostly tended to itself, but she had to check to make sure there were no invasive species creeping in to choke the life out of her friends.

She paused to admire a spider weaving her web when the purple bellflowers began to chime in alarm. Cilia brushed off her hands on her overalls and stood, wandering over to the blooms. "What's wrong, lovelies?"

Their leaves rustled, *Lost, lost, lost.*

"Lost? Hmm." Cilia turned to inspect her garden, its overflowing profusion of plants lovingly tended. The plants were a bit alarmist, truth be told. They often lost track of her cats and became concerned. However, Cilia could see Pine's black fur and Fig's brown mottled coat from where they dozed in the sun on her back porch.

"Such nonsense," she informed the bellflowers. "The cats are just sleeping."

Lost, lost, lost, chimed the bellflowers still. Further down, the twinflowers also took up the call. Then the thistles, then the sorrels, until it spread until her entire garden was telling her that something was lost.

"Enough, enough," Cilia said, raising her hands. "Just tell me where to find it."

The plants settled down, until it was just the yellow coneflowers far at the back of her garden. Cilia strode along the meandering slate stone path through the flowers, which shivered in greeting at her passage. When she arrived at the still rustling flowers, she put her hands on her hips and asked them, "What is it?"

The flowers settled and bent to show her a patch of dirt. Cilia frowned and crouched down and saw something entirely out of place. A gold ring lay in the dirt and she knew for certain it wasn't hers.

She picked it up and inspected it, hoping for some sort of clue as to who it belonged to. It was perfectly smooth, with no markings to tell her who had lost it. Cilia wasn't sure how it had gotten into her garden — the plants would have told her if someone had walked through them.

Just then, Cilia felt a tap on her shoulder. Startled, she stood up rapidly and found herself face to face with a young woman with eyes as dark as the twilight woods, her hair a dark mess of curls, her skin the colour of cedar bark.

"You found my ring," the woman said. "Thank you. I was trapped for a long time. Your plants have spent months using their roots to dig me up."

"Oh, you're welcome," Cilia said and held out the ring. "I'm happy these troublemakers could help. They're quite feisty when they want to be."

The yellow coneflowers rustled indignantly.

"Oh shush, you silly lot," Cilia said to the flowers and they quieted.

The stranger took the gold ring and reverently slid it on her finger. A ripple of gold light spread over her skin until she was suffused with it, before the light faded gently into her skin. The woman smiled. "They're lovely."

The coneflowers moved as if preening under the praise. Cilia sighed, knowing they would be lording that compliment over the other flowers in the garden for weeks.

Hoping to avert more trouble with her flowers, Cilia asked, "Would you like some tea?"

"Yes," the young woman said. "That would be nice." "This way then. My name's Cilia by the way," she said and started following the meandering path through the garden back to her cheery home.

"You can call me Marigold," the stranger said.

Cilia nodded, noting the specific phrasing.

Cilia led Marigold to her small stone patio, with its set of folding chairs and small metal table. Fig and Pine stretched and yawned, their pink tongues curling behind white teeth, and came over to investigate the new arrival.

"Be polite," Cilia instructed the cats and they merrowed in response, before sniffing Marigold. The stranger seemed delighted by them, holding out her hands for them to smell before stroking their sun-warmed fur.

Cilia stepped into her home, kicking off her clogs and padding barefoot into the kitchen. She put the kettle to boil and pulled out a selection of teas. She settled on a nice soothing chamomile and hummed as she arranged the teapot and cups on a tray with the sugar bowl and milk pitcher. When it was all ready, she carried the tray out and placed it gently on the table in front of Marigold. She found that Fig, the fluffy suck, had found a space on Marigold's lap and had curled up purring, while Pine was curled at her feet.

"Your cats are funny," Marigold said, "they say you're a witch."

"A witch!" Cilia snorted. "Hardly. Just a little trickle of power here and there to make green things grow."

Marigold accepted a teacup and spooned several helpings of sugar into her cup before pouring the tea in. "A green witch, then. I have been asleep for many years, but I am pleased to share tea with one of your kind."

"I don't mean to be rude," Cilia said, pouring her own cup, "but what are you? How did your ring end up in my garden?"

Marigold smiled and put down her cup for a moment. She closed her eyes and hummed a singular note, and Cilia's vision distorted. For a moment, she saw golden wings as fine as spiderwebs sprouting from Marigold's back, Marigold's pointed teeth, her face inhumanely shaped, her eyes entirely black. Then the hummed note stopped and Cilia blinked her eyes. "A fae? I thought you were all extinct."

"Extinct?" Marigold asked, her face falling. "You mean I have been asleep so long that I am the last of my kind?"

Cilia paused, considering her words. "Magic has been bleeding from our world slowly but surely. Your kind have not been seen in many years. It's possible the fae are still alive in hidden places, but I don't know of them."

Marigold sipped her tea. Her shoulders slumped. "I am tied to my ring. It was stolen from me by a man who thought he might have me for his bride, but a faerie's ring is a curse to the bearer if it is taken by force. He must have been killed where your garden stands now and the ring became buried in the earth. I slept while it remained so. When you touched it, you awoke me."

"Oh," Cilia said. "Do you have a home to go back to?"

Marigold paused, her cup hovering in the air. "I don't know. I hadn't thought about it. Maybe not?"

Cilia took a deep breath and took a sip of tea to steel her nerves. "Well, since you're here, I've got a couch, and you're welcome to stay with me as long as you like, until you decide where you want to go. My cats already like you."

"Really?" Marigold beamed. "I would like that! Thank

you, Cilia."

Cilia hid a blush by taking another long sip of her tea. "No problem. It is my pleasure to host a fae."

Marigold leaned forward with a secret smile. "It is my honour to stay with a green witch who tends to the gardens of the world."

Cilia's cheeks flamed bright red and she murmured half-strangled words about Marigold exaggerating.

Marigold's eyes danced with laughter and she took a sip of tea, the ring on her finger flashing in the sunlight.

Rage of Creation

We walked through a forest of glass that over the decades had begun to drip. Glass was, after all, neither a solid nor a liquid, but something caught perfectly in between. No two ancient spires of glass were the same. Some were tall, others no more than tripping hazards. None of them were perfectly smooth, however. They were all jagged or crooked or spiked, like a mad sculptor had poured only rage into their creation.

One might mistakenly think that this was beautiful, but on experiencing this alien maze of glass as far as the eye can see for themselves, they would quickly change their minds.

The sun was unrelenting overhead, and the light

caught and fractalled and reflected in all of the glass. We wore special goggles to shield our eyes, we covered our skin in cloth to prevent burns, but there was no escaping the furnace of heat that we travelled through. We were all sweating, exhausted, thirsty, craving shade and cool water.

Three days into a journey with an uncertain outcome and an unknown path ahead of us. No one before us had survived this hellish place to tell of it. We found evidence of others who had attempted the crossing before, now dried husks undisturbed by scavengers, still wrapped in clothes and sitting or lying where they had fallen. They were perfectly preserved in the dry heat of this place, a warning to all others who might seek to cross the expanse of glass.

They were driven by the same foolish hope that we clutched to our hearts as the five of us trudged onwards, seeking the end of the glass. It is told that it was the great dragons of old who created this place, burning the sands of a desert with dragon fire so hot it formed the maze. The stories say that the dragons did it to protect a fabled city, where magic flows like water and the people are all young and healthy and pure.

Our people, cursed by the dragons for a long ago wrong we had committed, were fading away, doomed to be lost to the sands of time. Unless we could reach the city at the heart of this godsforsaken place and beg the people there to help us, save us if they can. What use is fountains of magic and eternal youth if they cannot use it in the service of others?

I am not too proud to beg. Each of us who was sent is the last youth of one of the five remaining family lines. We cannot conceive more. If we die here in this unforgiving place, the hopes of our people die with us. So we continue, onwards, the burden of the survival of hundreds resting on our aching shoulders. I do not know what we will find. I only hope it will be the revival of our people.

The days pass. The sun and the stars wheel overhead. First one, then another, then another, fall to the heat and the despair of the unending glass maze. They fall or they sit and simply never rise again. Then it is just me.

I am alone.

I walk, stumbling now, barely able to see in front of me. The world has faded to the five feet in front of my shoes, which are barely holding together from the glass and the rough sand that scours them. My water is low. Perhaps a day, perhaps two. Then this place will take me too.

I keep on. I will fight until the end.

I walk, I rest, I walk, I rest.

I forget what drove me to this place. The only thing I

can think of is escape. To escape into cool darkness, shade, water. Sleep.

It takes me time to notice that the ground in front of me has changed. There's grass, green and jarring against my partially blinded eyes. I collapse to my knees, tearing off my goggles, and weep with my face pressed against the growing green earth.

I stretch out on the grass, running the sharp blades between my fingers in wonder, not caring where I am, other than free. Free of the torment of the glass and the oppressive heat.

Soft footsteps surround me and then gentle hands are picking me up, but I cannot see well; the sun strikes at my eyes and I close them, letting the hands carry me away, too exhausted to fight them.

I surrender.

When I resurface, I'm in a dark room lying on something soft. I've been bathed and a loose nightgown covers me. Something cold and weighted lies over my eyes but it feels nice, so I leave it. I touch my face and I can feel the peeling skin, the heat radiating from the burns, but it doesn't hurt. I sink back under.

I come to once again, and this time I can sit up. My eyes

open, but I can only see dim grey shapes. It's enough to recognize that I am lying on a bed. My body is weak and my tongue thick with thirst. I call out hoarsely, "Hello?"

Soft shuffling footsteps respond and there's the sound of a curtain being drawn back. I can make out the shape of a heavy-set figure, a white apron against grey clothing. The figure draws near and leans in, examining my face. I can make out a round face, gentle green eyes, a button nose, crooked lips. "Hello there, I'm Fran Foster. You can call me Fran. You've been asleep for a long time, no surprise. How are you feeling?"

"Thirsty," I croak, raising a hand to my throat as if it could ease the ache.

Fran bustles away, returns with a cup that she presses into my hands. Shakily, I raise it to my lips, and gulp at the cool liquid gratefully.

"Your eyes are looking better," she comments. "Can you see?"

I let the half-full cup hover for a moment and say, "Some."

She makes a tsking sound, and settles down on the foot of the bed. "A pity that. Not surprising, having gone through the Glass Forest. Not many come by that way, but those that do are always worse for the wear. What's your name?"

I take a drink of cool water and sigh deeply. "William. My name is William."

"What on earth sent you through that horrible maze? You look very young. You didn't go by yourself, did you?"

My throat still aches, but the words are easier now. "No. There were…five of us. I am the last."

Memory comes flooding back, of the others falling one by one to the heat, stopping and not rising again. The desperate hope that drove us. I drop the empty cup and clutch at Fran's arm. "You have to help my people. You have magic don't you? Eternal youth and fountains. Please help us."

Fran laughs. "The heat must have scrambled your brain. Magic? We don't have magic here. What are you talking about?"

"No magic?" I repeat hoarsely. "No magic?"

Cold settles around my bones. It was all for nothing. My people will die. I curl my knees to my chest and wrap my arms around them.

"Where are you from, anyways?"

"The other side of the glass. We were the Gha'ti'lin. We were cursed, and now we will all die."

"That's a little dramatic, don't you think," Fran says gently. "I haven't heard of your people before, but we don't cross the Forest. I'm sure they'll be fine."

I bury my face in my arms and mumble, "There are no more children. We were the last. We were sent for help."

Fran rests a gentle hand on my elbow. "There now, you're safe here. We'll take care of you."

"But my family. My people. They will all die. There will be none left."

"We cannot go through the Forest either. I'm sorry for your loss."

The tears come then, hot and heavy. I shake with the weight of them, the weight of knowing that I will be the last of my people. Fran stands and I hear her footsteps fading away into the distance.

Alone, alone, always alone. I will always be alone.

Deer, Leaping

A deer leaped and a car crashed.

I asked God why. I asked him what I had done to deserve the pain and anguish, why I deserved to feel such loss. I asked him if praying to him every Sunday since I was a little girl was not enough, if he had expected more from me, if maybe he had felt I had been insincere or sinful in some way that I was not aware of.

I wept in anger when he did not answer me, I raged against Him and everything he was, I screamed he wasn't being fair. I shunned my church; I offered no prayer except a demand for an explanation. My pastor came to visit and told me that God works in mysterious ways and that he has a purpose for everything and everyone. I politely thanked him and told him I'd only return to the congregation when I was ready.

I didn't care if God had a code to follow that only he understood; I am a lowly mortal and need something more solid to grasp than vague sentiments of higher intentions. I need to see purpose, for it to mean something.

A deer leaped and a car crashed. The deer was young, female, and the car was blue, hatchback.

I tried to bargain with the Fates.

A deer leaped and a car crashed. The deer was young, female, and the car was blue, hatchback. There was a horrible screech of tires and squealing of brakes followed by a sharp heavy bang and the splintering of glass. In the aftermath, there was only the purring of an idle engine.

I wished I could go back in time to tell that deer not to cross the road.

A deer leaped and a car crashed. The deer was young, female, and the car was blue, hatchback. There was a horrible screech of tires and squealing of brakes followed by a sharp heavy bang and the splintering of glass. In the aftermath, there was only the purring of an idle engine. The screaming sirens of the ambulance took exactly six minutes and twenty-two seconds to arrive on scene after 911 was dialled. They found a man inside the car, head tilted at an unnatural angle with the doe's head resting on his shoulder, limpid eyes apologetic.

I wondered if I could have told Rob to stay home just a few minutes longer, so that the deer could have crossed the road and he could have made it to work and I never would have received the phone call that crushed my heart. If only I could have convinced him to finish his coffee, not to hurry for his meeting, stolen a long kiss as he put on his jacket, if he would have stopped and stayed just long enough not to hit the deer.

A deer leaped and a car crashed. The deer was young, female, and the car was blue, hatchback. There was a horrible screech of tires and squealing of brakes followed by a sharp heavy bang and the splintering of glass. In the aftermath, there was only the purring of an idle engine. The screaming sirens of the ambulance took exactly six minutes and twenty-two seconds to arrive on scene after 911 was dialled. They found a man inside the car, head tilted at an unnatural angle with the doe's head resting on his shoulder, limpid eyes apologetic. There was nothing they could do for either; the man rode stiff and cold in the back of the ambulance to the morgue, the deer jostled in the back of a pickup truck to an unmarked grave.

I sat quietly, having no one left to be angry with, and nothing left to wonder about. I folded my hands and promised myself I would never stop loving Rob, no matter how much it hurt. I forgave.

Not My Home

Inspired by the memoirs of World War 1 volunteer ambulance driver Edward R. Coyle and the experiences of the people of Badonviller.

"They shot him! They shot him!"

Marie was hysterical, her clawed hands clutching at her chest, repeating the same three words over and over. She nearly broke down my door with her fist in her frantic grief, and I couldn't even invite her across my threshold before she began wailing.

I awkwardly pulled my lifelong friend into a hug, murmuring softly that her son had died a brave death fighting the Germans. I didn't believe it for a minute; there was nothing brave about dying, regardless of who her son had been fighting. I don't know if she heard me, but she quieted and sobbed onto my shoulder. I rocked her gently, rubbing her back to calm her down. Over the sound of her sobbing, I could hear the staccato bursts of gunfire in the near distance being exchanged between our boys and the Boches.

They won't be able to hold them off forever, crossed my thoughts. Dread crept in from the corner of my mind where I had locked it up. I desperately wanted to find somewhere quiet, where I could sit and pretend that the Germans weren't going to destroy our town. I didn't want to deal with the woman sobbing on me, whose problems at the moment were dwarfed by the larger future looming ahead. "Marie, you should go see to your husband. He lost his son too. And your daughter, she lost her brother."

She sniffled and looked at me, her eyes red and swollen. "You're right, Pauline. I've left them too long. Oh, my poor boy!"

Breaking into fresh tears, she pulled away from me. She gathered up the hem of her skirt and ran back down the streets to her home, where her nineteen-year-old son no doubt lay on the kitchen table, eyes closed, skin too pale, clothes stained a dark red.

I sighed, and leaned heavily against the door to my home. My husband and my two boys had enlisted already, and I hadn't heard from them since they left, which I took as a good sign. No news was good news in this case.

"They won't have to witness our home being destroyed," I commented to myself. I shivered and stepped back inside. After latching the door, I hugged myself and went to the kitchen, where I'd left a blanket. Wrapping it around my shoulders, I sat down at the wooden table, staring at the dark surface.

I could almost pretend that I didn't hear the clatter and snap of gunfire.

I woke up in the middle of the night, feeling uneasy. Sitting up, I listened to the darkness for a moment. There was no more gunfire, but a strange repetitive thumping. Cautiously, I went to the window and peered through a crack in the shutters.

In the darkness, a steady stream of German soldiers was marching through the village, five men shoulder to shoulder in the street, their boots stepping in sync.

This was it. This was the end.

"Kaffee!"

I shuddered at the sound of the Surgeon's shout above my head. I put aside the broom I'd been using to sweep the floor and kept my head down under the contemptuous gaze of the German officers occupying my sitting room. Maps and papers were taking up every available surface, rendering the room nearly unrecognizable. I understood little of what they were saying, but I knew the call for more coffee.

I shuffled into the kitchen and checked the pot. It was still hot to the touch, and I used a fold of my skirt to keep my hand from burning to pour the dark, rich liquid into a cup. It steamed readily, and I almost could smell a whiff of the coffee before the stench of the human remains piled outside my house won the battle for the air. Ignoring the smell which I'd had to live with for days since the French forces had rallied and pushed back against the Huns, I carefully climbed the stairs to the rooms that had become an impromptu hospital. Specialty: amputation.

As I climbed the stairs, the stench of rotting took on a new queasy note of sickness and dying. I had to hold up the hem of my skirts to prevent them from brushing against the men who lay on mats or sat propped up everywhere, mumbling and whimpering, twitching in fever dreams. I had to swallow revulsion; these strangers were pitiful, but I couldn't summon even a small amount of compassion for them. They were in my house against my will, they were destroying my country, they'd killed my youngest son with artillery shells, and they'd shot Marie in cold blood when she stood sobbing outside her house during their victory march through town.

They deserved to suffer, I thought viciously.

The man I knew only as the Surgeon was muttering to himself, checking bandages, when he looked up and saw me. "Ah, endlich!"

He plucked the cup from my hand and downed it in a few gulps, swearing under his breath when it burned his tongue. He gave me a passing glance as he thrust the cup back at me and commented in near-perfect French, "Coffee smells much better than the sick."

I knew an opportunity when I saw one. "Well, maybe, if I could clean the courtyard outside, it wouldn't smell so bad…"

The Surgeon scowled at me, his dark brows knitting together in consternation. "Scheiß Frau! Kannst du nicht sehen dass wir sind beschäftigt? Get out of my sight, or else we will be tossing *you* out the window!"

I clutched the cup to my chest and ducked my head, nearly running as I left the room, terrified that he'd change his mind and hurl me out the window along with the latest amputated limb, to land bent and broken on the pile of arms and legs that lay in my courtyard. As I hurried away, desperate hands clutched at my skirts, begging in a language I didn't understand; maybe for kindness or mercy or death, I wasn't sure, but I couldn't have helped them even had I wanted to.

Down the stairs and back in my kitchen, I realised my knuckles were white and aching from how tightly I was clutching the coffee cup. Putting it down, I tucked my hands in my skirt pockets to stop them from trembling. I don't know how long it was that I was standing in the kitchen, trying to stop thinking about the death which surrounded me, when one of the Boche officers came into the kitchen, and gave me a sharp slap on the arm.

"Lazy French bitch! You're not done sweeping! You think you can stand here all day and do nothing? Get back to work!" He punctuated each phrase with another slap. My face felt hot with tears as I returned to being a slave in my own house. If only this damned war would end.

Frozen in the Dark

It is quiet. Or at least, it is quiet in comparison to the chaos of the day.

Even the enemy needs sleep, but it isn't a peaceful night. Waiting clung to everything, heavy and stifling in the darkness. Every crack of a branch is a sniper's shot, every flicker of a leaf in the wind is the enemy advancing. Rain pours down in steady sheets, granting no reprieve from the mud and the cold. At least the artillery guns are quiet. At least.

Four soldiers huddle together shoulder to shoulder to stay warm on the leeward side of a hill, the black outlines of twisted trees sheltering them. They pass a cigarette between them, the single dot of red flaring then dimming again with every inhale. The rain takes on a tinny tone as it hits their helmets, a pausing place before trickling off the metal brims and dropping the last few feet to the muddy ground.

"I sure hope the lieutenant comes back soon," A private says quietly, shifting to adjust the way his rifle sits across his knees.

"He's probably lying dead with his face in the mud and some bastard pissing on him," A corporal, not the most optimistic by nature. "There's no way he's going to find the position we're supposed to be at in the dark. He probably tripped face first into a bayonet."

"Both of you shut up. I'm tired of hearing you both complain all the time." The sergeant, louder than the first two. He takes a drag of the cigarette and exhales a long breath of smoke.

"We're all going to die here. I hope they write on my grave, 'Died from rain and following orders'." The corporal again, wiping a sleeve across his face, smearing some of the mud that already obscures his features. "Asshole officers coming up with plans for multi-prong attacks in the dark."

"I want to go home." The private, whimpering. Definitely the youngest.

136

"Look, how 'bout this, in ten minutes, if the lieutenant isn't back, we strike out on our own," the sergeant says, practical.

"None of us have a watch." A fourth, silent until then. Another private, not as young as the first. "They're all broken or lost."

"I'll count in my head." The sergeant, with a sense of finality.

Silence.

The rain continues pattering on the branches and the ground and their helmets and their sodden coats. They shiver together in a massed clump, the cigarette used up, their rifles clutched in freezing fingers.

Then, movement in the darkness. The youngest private sees it first and nudges the corporal next to him, pointing a shaking finger.

The corporal squints, trying to make out the shape. The others, now alert, sit up and look towards where the private is pointing.

"What the fuck's that?" whispers the corporal.

The older private slowly aims his rifle towards the movement, cautious to make no sound. "A person."

The sergeant and the corporal train their guns on the target as well. The sergeant mutters, "Hard to tell if he's one of ours."

The shadowed shape stumbles through the trees a few hundred yards away, seemingly having trouble finding his way.

"I have a clear shot," says the older private. "Should I take it?"

"What if it's the lieutenant?" whispers the younger private.

The sergeant is quiet for a beat, weighing their options.

The corporal shifts to balance on the balls of his feet, crouched and ready. "I don't want to be wrong. If he's not one of ours, there could be more where he came from."

"The shot will alert everyone that we're here," the sergeant. "He might just pass us by."

The younger private shivers. "Do we wait?"

The form stumbles, struggles to rise, but then staggers upright and keeps going. He veers drunkenly.

"He's hurt." The older private still has his gun trained on the object of their attention. "Still can't tell the uniform. I think he's lost parts of it."

138

The sergeant lowers his rifle. "Take the shot."

There's a loud crack as a single bullet cuts through the rain. The figure falls to his knees, and after a moment hunched over, crumples sideways. There is stillness again, but for the rain.

The barrel of the private's rifle sizzles where the rain hits it, small puffs of steam rising.

"Should we check who it is?" The corporal.

The sergeant shakes his head. "No. The lieutenant's been gone too long, and we're not in position. Let's go."

The sergeant cautiously rises to his feet, water sluicing off the brim of his helmet. He slings his rifle over his shoulder and takes one more look at the fallen soldier still a distance away. The others follow, adjusting helmets and coats against the rain.

The sergeant leads them away, a strong sense of direction guiding his steps. The lieutenant had ordered them to stay in place while he recced the route. The sergeant was quite certain the lieutenant had no idea where he was going.

The other three soldiers fell in behind their sergeant, their faith placed on his shoulders as they stumbled over rocks and roots and mud in the darkness. The sergeant knew how to get them into position.

Not that it would keep any of them safe. Death trailed them like an expectant lover.

A Friend Eternal

It may have been a year and a day since It happened. Time lost meaning, but every day that passed without him engraved itself on her heart, a permanent scar. She still remembered It clearly: her dog, Anubis, crossing the street. Calling him to come back. The pickup that couldn't stop in time. Anubis' pitiful whining, his life bleeding out across the pavement, red on grey. His beautiful amber eyes that had once smiled at her, staring vacantly at the azure sky.

She had grieved for months. People told her to get over him, he was just a dog, she could buy another one. But, every time she went to a breeder or a shelter, she couldn't find him. She walked around the neighborhood trying to find him, hoping it had just been a terrible nightmare and he would come bounding up to her again, just as before. Everything could go back to the way it had been.

On her walks, she met other dogs with their owners, but she still couldn't find him. Once she thought she saw him crossing the street down the block, but when she ran to him, he wasn't there. Sometimes she saw flickers of him out of the corner of her eye. He haunted her every step. Sometimes when the grief crippled her, she liked to pretend that his soul had returned to be her guide.

She had tried dating for a time, but no man could fill the void of the selfless love Anubis had given her. He had not simply been a pet: he had been her best friend, her motivation, her life and her will. But he had left her so suddenly.

Today, she couldn't keep up the pretense of living anymore. She didn't leave her small apartment. She spent her time pacing back and forth, waiting for her lost half to return.

Time shifted. She forgot to eat. Day blended into night into day. People knocked on the door, but she didn't answer. Manila envelopes stamped "Urgent" were slipped under the door. She avoided touching them.

When she slept, she dreamed of him lying on his half

142

of the bed. He always seemed to want to tell her something, something *important*, but she couldn't understand. Every night, the dreams became clearer and clearer. She awoke in the morning feeling disorientated, not comprehending the cold emptiness of her bed.

One winter's night after she had fallen asleep exhausted, she awoke to a familiar sound. The faint scratching of nails against the door, accompanied by a high-pitched whine. She sat up in bed, elation filling her to the point where she wanted to clap her hands and scream with joy. No fear or suspicion clouded her mind as she flew on wings of love to the door. Her heart was pounding in her ears. The door was unlocked, *of course it was*, and swung open easily at her touch.

There he sat, tongue lolling out in a grin. Her darling Great Dane, her beloved Anubis.

She fell to her knees before him, and wrapped her arms around his neck, grabbing fistfuls of fur to reassure herself he was real. Tears ran down her cheeks as she inhaled his oh so familiar smell.

"Anubis," she breathed, "Anubis, love, you've come back to me." Memories flashed through her mind, as everything she had associated with him came back in a breath.

Sunbathing on the deck, the wind rippling his glossy blue-grey fur, playing in the autumn leaves, star gazing in cozy blankets, their first winter snowfall together, his sloppy puppy kisses… So much that she had lost when she had lost him. Time slowed to a crawl as he gently licked the salty tears off her face.

When her tears had run dry, she closed the door behind him. Anubis sat patiently, looking up at her with a wagging tail. She murmured softly, "What took you so long?"

He yawned in response, his tongue curling as it always did, and got to his feet to follow her. She turned on the lights to the kitchen and found his bag of kibble, but he ignored the offered bowl of food. He trotted away in disinterest to their bedroom, his nails clicking on the hardwood. He jumped up onto the bed gracefully and curled up on his half. She turned off the lights and joined him, crawling under the covers next to him, his deep breathing lulling her into sleep.

Her dreams, however, were not comforting. She dreamt she awoke to find Anubis gone and a pile of manila envelopes on the floor. This dream couldn't be shaken off, no matter how hard she tried, until she broke down in tears and cried herself into oblivion. She awoke once again to Anubis' warm presence, and reached out to him as a child reaches to its mother. He blinked open one liquid amber eye, then the other. He yawned, and for no reason at all, she smiled. He was home.

She stayed in bed the entire morning, Anubis beside her. He made her feel blissfully happy, simply by being present. She walked with him in the afternoon, in the abandoned streets of midsummer. They found a grassy hill to lie on and basked in the sun. She closed her eyes.

She must have dozed off because when she woke up dark clouds had gathered overhead, she was covered in a dusting of snow, and the wind bit into her exposed skin. Shivering, she didn't understand what had happened. She sat up and looked around, but she could no longer see Anubis. She whistled for him, but he didn't answer. Frozen and hungry, she started to walk back to her apartment. Halfway there, it started to snow heavily, and despite the futility, she ran the rest of the way.

She was cold to the bone by the time she came to her door, and once inside, she immediately stripped off her summer clothes and left them in a pile with the manila envelopes. After trying to flick on the lights and finding that the switch didn't work, she thought there must have been a power outage. She crawled into bed and curled up to try and stay warm, wishing the electricity was working. She drifted off to sleep, waiting for Anubis to return to her.

When she awoke once more, she found he was asleep next to her, his head resting on her shoulder. Golden sunlight streamed through her window, dappling his fur in light. She watched his nose twitch in his dreams. She wondered what he was dreaming about. She dozed again.

She was caught in her nightmare again. She paced the dark apartment naked, shivering, waiting for Anubis. Eventually, she lay down on her bed in her dream, feeling weak and hungry.

When she next woke up, the first rays of sun were filtering into her bedroom. She sat up, rummaged through her dresser for jeans and a t-shirt, and dressed herself in front of the floor-length mirror. There were soft clicks against the hardwood as Anubis joined her in looking into the mirror.

She knelt beside him, and wrapped an arm around him.

"Why do you always leave me?" she asked him, looking at him.

Anubis gazed back into her eyes steadily, an uncanny intelligence in his regard. When she could no longer meet his eyes, unsettled by their intensity, she looked back at the mirror.

She thought she might be dreaming. Instead of the bedroom reflecting back at her, there was snow and ancient towering pines whose branches threatened to black out the sky. Flakes of snow were lazily falling down from the white sky, collecting on her auburn hair and in Anubis' glistening fur.

She raised a trembling hand to her mouth, watching her reflection in the mirror imitate her. She closed her eyes, gripping Anubis' fur in her hands tightly, trying to understand what she was seeing.

"Do not fear." The voice that spoke was deep and rumbling, with a certain inhumanity in its tone. She opened her eyes, avoiding looking at the mirror.

"What?" She wasn't sure to whom she was talking, but she looked at Anubis as she asked her question.

"You are seeing home," Anubis seemed to say. His voice was gentle.

"Oh," she said, and allowed herself to glance into the mirror. *Home?* Well, it didn't seem so bad now. In fact, it looked almost inviting.

She wondered if there was a smell of wood smoke, or the chittering of hardy winter birds. Her reflection smiled at her and flickered slightly to be wearing winter clothes. She gaped at the mirror in shock.

"Good, you are seeing how you could be. My love, stretch your mind further, and I will no longer be bound to this form you have given me." She felt dazed and suddenly quite faint. Her vision started fading, the colours of the mirror muting. She panicked and wrapped her arms tightly around Anubis. Everything went black.

When her vision came back, she was lying on the floor, naked. She realized it was her nightmare again. Feeling weak and trapped, she rasped out, "Anubis?"

The only answer was the echoed word off the silent, unfeeling walls. She started to sob and pulled herself towards the mirror. She touched it cautiously with a finger, but found it to be cold and unyielding. *This is just a dream, it'll end, it has to…*

She pressed her palm against the mirror. It stolidly showed her a sickly husk of herself, but would not show her what she wanted to see. Anger and frustration welled up inside and she slapped her hand against the mirror. Her hand stung, but that only added to her anger. Snarling viciously, she pounded her fists against the mirror, feeling perversely satisfied when it cracked and shattered into a rain of glittering shards. Glass surrounded her, pierced her skin. Clutching her bleeding hands and wrists to her chest, she prayed for her nightmare to end.

No matter how tightly she closed her eyes and willed herself to wake up, it persisted. She started shivering as sweat dried and cooled on her fevered skin. She clawed at her skin, her face, her hair, desperate for anything that would let her escape this nightmare. Blood was running down her chest, pooling in her navel, but she didn't care.

Her tongue felt like sandpaper in her mouth, and her stomach was no more than an empty void consuming itself, but the dream would not give her up. Wailing with desperation, she keeled over onto her side. Her throat was dry, and her wail turned to a croak and then silence. She could only stare numbly at her wrists, watching blood run down from the embedded shards of glass and pool on the hardwood.

It was sweet relief when she found herself awake once more. She shook off the memory of her nightmare, and looked around. She didn't see Anubis, and puzzled, stood up. The mirror was whole, and showing her what Anubis had called home. Her reflection was dressed in a fur-trimmed coat, her glossy curls spilling neatly out of the hood and down to her chest. Her reflection smiled at her and held out a beckoning hand.

She swallowed, wanting to take that hand and become this woman, untouched by pain. But, she could not see Anubis, and she would not leave without him.

"I am here." A dignified man stepped into her line of sight. He was tall, with short black hair, dark angular features, and soft amber eyes. He moved with a flowing, feral grace that was immediately familiar.

"My love," she whispered. He smiled at her and wrapped his arm loosely around her reflection's waist.

"Join me, my love. There is no longer any need to be afraid." His words soothed her, and she tentatively reached towards her reflection's outstretched hand. Her fingers felt as if they passed through cool water before her hand met her reflection's. Her arm started to tingle as the mirror tugged her in deeper. She took a step in, passing farther through the cool curtain.

Half in, half out, she could hear her heart beating in her ears. There was a faint echo of someone else's heartbeat she could hear. Dimly she was aware of someone shouting, "Wake up, Nancy! Oh my god, the paramedics, phone the paramedics! She's bleeding to death!" It sounded like her landlady. She hesitated.

Anubis smiled encouragingly at her. The second heartbeat grew louder, and she realized it was his. The beats sped up, to keep time with her own heart. Were there two separate hearts? It did not matter, for they were beating as one, were one.

She stepped completely through the mirror, feeling cleansed by the coolness as she passed through. She felt a cold breeze sting her cheeks and the warmth of a strong arm around her waist. When she opened her eyes, she was looking into a bedroom where a stranger lay on the ground. There were people all around the bloody stranger, with white gauze, blue gloves. They pressed two pads to the woman's chest, and she arched from the shock. They tried again and the woman was convulsing. Shards of a broken mirror glittered around the pale woman, speckled with bright red. And then everything went black.

She could hear a heartbeat.

Lub-dub…lub-dub…

She recognized her own heartbeat. *Why is it slowing down?* She willed it to beat faster, but it wouldn't.

…lub…dub…lub…

I must be dying.

..dub…lub…

Why?

..dub…lub…

Anubis…love…

…dub.

Acknowledgement

No book would be complete without proper thanks given. I have to start by saying thank you to Chris, who helped me capture exactly what I wanted to say in the introductory statement. Another thank you goes to Charlene, who answered my numerous publishing questions. My unending gratitude go to Nick, Lauren, and Justine, for being such amazing friends and supporters of my writing. Pat, thank you for your insights — you solved a major question for me. The staff of Salt and Sage Books made the editing process relatively painless, and helped me see these stories in a new light.

Sea Borne was previously published in Blind Corner Literary Magazine. Some of the other stories have previously been shared in shorter unedited form on Instagram in response to prompts. I am grateful for every writing community I have had the chance to be a part of, whether digital or in person, as there's nothing more inspiring than a group of people with a shared passion.

About the Author

Myka Silber grew up surrounded by the forests, mountains, and ocean of the Pacific Northwest. They now live in Ontario, Canada, with a mercurial cat and a bean of a dog. Myka holds both a BA and an MA in International Relations. They have previously published a short story collection and a novel, and you can follow them on Instagram @myka.silber.